WELCOME TO
THE COW TOWN WHERE
THE STREETS RUN RED WITH BLOOD!

LUKE TRAVIS: A lawman with a fast gun and a steely eye, he knows the value of restraint—until a war party gallops into Abilene . . .

AILEEN BLOOM: The beautiful doctor has a fighter's courage when it comes to healing—and saving lives . . .

CODY FISHER: Brave and bold, the young deputy puts his life on the line for the half-breed whose presence threatens Abilene . . .

WHITE ELK DUQUESNE: Son of a French-American father and a Kiowa mother, he's deadly with both knife and gun. Now he's facing a showdown with a warrior whose hatred burns hot . . .

BUFFALO KNIFE: White Elk's boyhood friend is now his sworn enemy, seeking blood vengeance at any price . . .

SERGEANT VIRGIL DRAKE: A boozy, brawling cavalry officer, his fight with the half-breed is not one of honor, but of revenge. He begins with White Elk's woman . . .

RITA NEVINS: One of Abilene's working girls, she's a blond lady of the night with a weakness for White Elk—and a passion to save his life . . .

Books by Justin Ladd

Abilene Book 1: The Peacemaker
Abilene Book 2: The Sharpshooter
Abilene Book 3: The Pursuers
Abilene Book 4: The Night Riders
Abilene Book 5: The Half-Breed

Published by POCKET BOOKS

Most Pocket Books are available at special quantity discounts for bulk purchases for sales promotions, premiums or fund raising. Special books or book excerpts can also be created to fit specific needs.

For details write the office of the Vice President of Special Markets, Pocket Books, 1230 Avenue of the Americas, New York, New York 10020.

JUSTIN LADD
ABILENE

Book 5

THE HALF-BREED

 BCI ™ Created by the producers of
Wagons West, Stagecoach,
White Indian, and San Francisco.

Book Creations Inc. Canaan, NY. Lyle Kenyon Engel, Founder

POCKET BOOKS

New York   London   Toronto   Sydney   Tokyo

This book is a work of fiction. Names, characters, places and incidents are either the product of the author's imagination or are used fictitiously. Any resemblance to actual events or locales or persons, living or dead, is entirely coincidental.

An *Original* Publication of POCKET BOOKS

POCKET BOOKS, a division of Simon & Schuster Inc.
1230 Avenue of the Americas, New York, NY 10020

ISBN: 0-671-66990-7

First Pocket Books printing December 1988

10 9 8 7 6 5 4 3 2 1

POCKET and colophon are trademarks of
Simon & Schuster Inc.

Printed in the U.S.A.

Prologue

AN EARLY MORNING FOG SHROUDED THE LOW HILLS of the Kiowa reservation in Indian Territory and cloaked the scattered buildings in eerie gray shadows. The sun, hovering just below the horizon, would soon rise to quickly burn away the mist and usher in another warm late spring day. But now all was quiet and dim among the buildings and lodges scattered across the broad valley.

On the edge of the Kiowa settlement sat several simple wooden buildings used by the Indian agent and the small garrison of soldiers stationed on the reservation. There was a house for the agent and his wife, a meeting hall, a long barracks building for the soldiers, and a large barn with a pole corral behind it. The garrison's mounts stood calmly grazing in the corral. A sleepy-eyed private came from the barn carrying a bucket of water. He trudged toward the trough at the edge of the corral with his head down, just like the horses in his charge.

As the morning breeze shifted, one of the animals, scenting something unusual, abruptly lifted its head. Another horse snorted; several more pawed the ground and stamped. At first the trooper did not notice the warning signs as he sleepily went about his tasks. But one of the horses whinnied next to him, and he was at last aware of the animals' nervous behavior.

With a puzzled frown, the private looked up, slowly turned his head, and peered into the mist. He saw only the Army buildings, the Kiowa lodges beyond, and the isolated lodge that housed the visiting Army scout, Falling Moon. Everything appeared normal; even the dogs seemed to be asleep.

Suddenly, a warrior brandishing a knife sprang from his hiding place behind the water trough. He lunged at the soldier, slashing viciously with the blade in his hand.

Reacting instinctively, the private swung the water bucket at the attacking Indian with one hand and desperately clawed at the service revolver strapped to his hip with the other. The holster's flap was snapped closed, and the stiff fastening resisted his scrabbling fingers.

The Kiowa's blade sliced deeply into the soldier's forearm. As blood spurted from the bone-deep gash, the private dropped the water bucket and opened his mouth to scream. Whirling behind the soldier, the Indian clamped his free hand over the struggling man's mouth to stifle the sound and then slashed the knife savagely across his throat. The trooper's eyes rolled, and his body sagged heavily against his murderer. Wiping his blade clean on the dead man's tunic, the Indian disdainfully shoved the body to the ground.

His dark eyes glittered with satisfaction as he turned and gestured with the weapon in his hand. At the signal, a dozen warriors appeared as if by magic from their hiding places and ran to the tall, commanding figure of their leader. "Yes, Buffalo Knife," one of the warriors muttered.

Sliding his blade into its leather sheath, Buffalo Knife knelt down and unbuckled the dead soldier's gun belt. As he straightened, he slung it around his hips and unsnapped the stiff holster flap. Later, when he had the time, he would saw off the flap to make the pistol more readily accessible.

Buffalo Knife looked at his men. "We take the weapons now," he said and gestured toward the barn.

The reservation had no armory; ammunition and spare rifles were stored in a locked room in the barn. Armed with the pistol, Buffalo Knife knew he would easily get past the lock.

He strode purposefully toward the barn, his dozen warriors following closely behind him. He was only a few feet from the open double doors when a sleepy-eyed trooper appeared there. The shirtless man was yawning and pulling his suspender straps over his long johns. When he saw the stony-faced Indian coming toward him, he froze.

In one smooth motion, Buffalo Knife swept the revolver from the holster, lifted it, and fired. The heavy slug punched into the trooper's forehead; its force flung him backward and dropped him to the ground. Buffalo Knife swiftly stepped over the corpse and moved into the barn. He had reached the door of the makeshift armory by the time the echo of the shot died away.

Another bullet smashed the lock. Buffalo Knife yanked the shattered lock away from the hasp, then kicked the door open. He stepped back to let his men move into the room and begin snatching up rifles and boxes of shells.

Less than a minute later, the band of renegades came out of the barn. All of them had used rifles before, and they were loading the stolen weapons with rapid, practiced fingers. One man hurried to the corral and began taking down the poles of the gate. As the others walked toward the agent's office, several soldiers scrambled out of the barracks, looking around wildly to find the source of the shots that had awakened them. Buffalo Knife snapped a command, and four of his braves opened fire.

The sudden volley surprised the soldiers and struck three of them before they knew where the shots were coming from. Grappling for their guns, the others frantically ducked into the barracks. They haphazardly returned the Indians' fire, but Buffalo Knife and his men had taken cover behind the meeting hall.

The Indian agent, dressed in his nightshirt, appeared in the doorway of his house. He stared at the band of Kiowa warriors for a long second, then turned and dove back into his home. Buffalo Knife fired his pistol at the empty doorway, the slug knocking splinters from the doorjamb. The Indian threw back his head and laughed. "Stay in your hole if you would live, rabbit!" he jeered.

His men moved quickly to both corners of the meeting hall and began shooting toward the barracks, keeping the soldiers pinned down. Suddenly, the thundering of hooves announced the release of the horses. Driven by the warrior Buffalo Knife had assigned to the task, the animals rushed out of the corral and came toward the meeting hall.

As the horses swept past, the warriors briefly stopped firing and hurtled after the animals. Clutching the flowing manes, they vaulted onto their backs and galloped away. Several of them triggered parting shots at the barracks.

Buffalo Knife was in the lead as the escaping renegades pounded toward the special lodge. This smaller lodge housed visiting Indian scouts who worked with the Army. As the fleeing braves approached it, Buffalo Knife saw two Indians armed with rifles running from it.

"I want Falling Moon alive!" he cried to his men over his shoulder. As his knees and heels guided his stolen mount with subtle pressure, he raised his pistol and triggered off two quick shots that spun one of the Indians to the ground. The other man hurriedly lifted his rifle and fired wildly toward the rapidly approaching band of Kiowa warriors. He did not have time to fire again before the renegades were upon him.

The man dodged desperately to his left to avoid one of the charging horses. As he did so, Buffalo Knife raced to his other side and lashed out with the pistol in his hand. The barrel cracked across the man's skull, and the Indian called Falling Moon crumpled to the ground.

As he swept on, Buffalo Knife shouted, "Bring the stinking Crow." One of the other braves slid off his horse and slung Falling Moon's body across the animal's back. Then the warrior remounted and galloped after his companions.

The renegades raced toward the Kiowa lodges, the noise of their passage awakening those who had not already been roused by the gunfire. As the stolen Army horses thundered past the lodges, some of the old men raised their hands and began chanting prayers to speed the young men on their way. The days of fighting the white men were over for most of the braves on this reservation, but clearly some of the young ones still had spirit.

Buffalo Knife leaned against the neck of his racing horse and pressed his legs into the animal's flanks. Speed was essential now. Sooner or later, the white soldiers would round up the rest of their horses and pursue the escaping warriors. He must consider the singing wires, too. The telegraph would quickly spread the tale of today's events, and all the yellowlegs in Indian Territory would be hunting for Buffalo Knife and his band of murdering renegades.

For that was what the Army would call them, and the white chiefs in charge of the soldiers would wish to make an example of them. They would either kill the Kiowas or bring them back to the reservation in chains, whichever would shame them the most. The white chiefs believed that would keep other Indians from trying to regain their freedom.

Buffalo Knife did not care about that. Let the white chiefs try to shame the Indians, and let the old men talk of the old days. He had something else—more important—to do. All he wanted was a weapon in his hand and a good horse between his legs. Those were the tools he needed for the vengeance he sought.

Buffalo Knife drove the fleeing band of renegades with their captive away from the reservation until the sun was high overhead and beat relentlessly down upon them. During the morning, Falling Moon had regained consciousness, but Buffalo Knife did not permit him to ride normally. He was kept slung over the back of a horse. His hands were lashed to his ankles under the animal's belly so that he could not cause trouble for the horse's rider.

By the time Buffalo Knife ordered a short halt, he knew that Falling Moon would not only fear for his life, he would be as sick as a dog as well.

The band stopped in a grove of cottonwoods beside a small creek. The braves dismounted and cared for their horses, allowing them to drink the cool, clear water. Then they drew water for themselves and sat in the shade to eat some of the jerky they carried while they waited for their leader to conclude his business.

Buffalo Knife positioned two men at the edge of

the grove to act as sentries. Then he ordered two others to take the captured Army scout from the horse, strip him, and stake him to the ground. As Falling Moon struggled, moaned, and whimpered, the Kiowa leader stood nearby and watched scornfully. The lack of dignity and courage disgusted him; the Crow had lived too long near the white men. He had forgotten what all Indians were born knowing—how to die.

When Falling Moon was tied down, Buffalo Knife slipped his blade from its sheath and knelt beside the naked Crow. "I have no time to enjoy this, dog," Buffalo Knife hissed. "The yellow-legs will be coming sooner than I would like. So tell me what I wish to know, and you shall die quickly."

Falling Moon spat a curse at the Kiowa leaning over him.

Buffalo Knife smiled thinly. He had been hoping that the Crow would not tell him what he wanted to know too soon.

With practiced fingers, Buffalo Knife began to work methodically on the Crow with his blade. As the steel became stained with crimson and Falling Moon's screams tore through the grove of trees, the Kiowa warriors sat impassively chewing on their jerky. All of them knew that the Crow had ridden for the white man's army as a scout. Whatever Buffalo Knife did to him would not be sufficient punishment for his treachery.

But there was one whom Buffalo Knife sought even more. One whose betrayal of his people could only be repaid with blood. Buffalo Knife leaned close to the whimpering Crow and hissed, "Where has he gone? He was your friend. You would know, dog!"

This time Falling Moon did not hesitate. "He rode north!" the Crow gasped. Blood bubbled from his mouth. As he tried to utter the next word, he choked. Buffalo Knife leaned even closer to hear the gurgling answer to his question.

Then, with one quick movement, he slit Falling Moon's throat.

At that moment, one of the sentries called out. The tall Kiowa stood up, stepped over the body of the Crow scout, and joined his sentry. Gazing back the way they had come, Buffalo Knife saw the dusty haze rising in the air.

"The yellowlegs come," he said, nodding solemnly. He had expected as much, but their pursuers were a long way behind them. He and his men were a small band, riding good horses that were now well rested. He knew they would easily slip away.

When the Kiowa band rode out of the grove of trees, Buffalo Knife left Falling Moon where he lay, as a warning to the soldiers who followed them. He knew that would not stop the white men. White men never knew when they were well off. They would keep coming. If Buffalo Knife and his men killed these pursuers, others would just take their place.

As he and his warriors rode north, he made a vow to the gods and to himself that he would stay free long enough to satisfy the hunger for revenge that had been gnawing at him ever since the defeat at the Battle of Palo Duro Canyon. He would kill the man who had betrayed him and all of his people.

All Buffalo Knife and his warriors had to do was reach the place called Abilene in Kansas. There they would find White Elk Duquesne.

Chapter One

———✦———

A TALL, DARK-HAIRED YOUNG MAN LEANED AGAINST
one of the boardwalk posts outside the Sunrise
Café and scanned Texas Street. His strong-
featured, lean face wore a somber expression, and
the grim impression he gave was reinforced by a
faint scar that ran diagonally across his right cheek.
He was dressed like any cowhand, in comfortable
range clothes, but had a different air. From the
flat-crowned hat on his head to the boots on his
feet, every article he wore was well cared for. The
shell belt and holster fastened around his hips were
made of well-oiled, supple black leather. Both the
ivory-handled Colt resting in the holster and the
badge pinned to his shirt gleamed in the morning
sun.

Deputy Cody Fisher had just finished his breakfast—steak, biscuits, eggs, and strong black coffee—and he knew he should be getting to work. But it was an especially nice morning in Abilene, and Cody had decided to savor it for a moment.

His rather forbidding appearance masked a keen intelligence, a quick wit, and a wealth of affection that he gave readily to his friends. Depending upon the situation, Cody could be a staunch ally or a deadly enemy. Now, as he relaxed against the post at the edge of the boardwalk, a smile began to play across his wide mouth.

The traffic on Texas Street was light this morning. A few men rode by on horseback, and an occasional farm wagon rolled down the hard-packed street. The dusty haze that would fill the air later in the day had not yet been kicked up.

Even at this hour, tinny music drifted through the batwings of the Old Fruit Saloon, several doors away. Most of the saloons in Abilene never closed. Although the vast herds of cattle were no longer being driven up from Texas to the railhead in Kansas, Abilene would always be a cow town at heart. The Great Western Cattle Company still maintained their stockyards on the eastern edge of town, and cowboys, either Texans or hands from some of the local ranches, were always on the streets of the city.

And Abilene *was* becoming a city, Cody thought as he looked at the buildings on Texas Street. There were plenty of saloons, but they stood storefront to storefront with general mercantile stores, hotels, and blacksmith shops. Dr. Aileen Bloom's office was just down the street, across from the apothecary and a milliner's shop. From where he stood he could see the roof of the red brick train depot, which was a couple of blocks north on Railroad Street. The tracks of the Kansas Pacific ran through the heart of Abilene, and near the depot were quite a few warehouses, a cotton gin, and two farm implement companies.

Civilization, Cody thought. *I'm not sure I like it.* Despite his youth, he had already been down some wild trails. Were it not for the badge, a stranger might have taken the young man for a gunfighter. In fact, Cody Fisher had been on that path when he had met Marshal Luke Travis. Since that day, Cody had worked for law and order, although his impulsive nature inspired him to bend the rules from time to time. He enjoyed his work and respected Luke Travis, but he was not certain he was ready for the settled life of a solid citizen just yet.

Those thoughts were running through Cody's head when a man riding down Texas Street from the west caught his eye. The stranger rode a fine-looking sorrel, but it was the buckskins he wore that attracted Cody's attention.

As the stranger drew closer, Cody saw that under his broad-brimmed hat he had a dark, handsome face and was young, probably in his mid-twenties. A pistol was holstered on his right hip, a bowie knife sheathed on the left. In a fringed buckskin boot attached to the saddle was a rifle. The young man was armed as if he expected trouble, and his wary, roving eyes contributed to the impression. Here was a man accustomed to riding in lonesome places, living on the fringes of the still-wild frontier, and depending on no one but himself for survival.

Cody could remember a time when he had been like that. Suddenly he wondered if living in a town, even with the frequent dangers he faced as a lawman, was taking the edge off his skills.

The stranger's searching eyes brushed over the deputy, then abruptly returned to him. As if he had found what he was looking for, the man swung his horse out of the center of the street and walked him toward the boardwalk. When he reined in, Cody noticed the stubble on his cheeks and the gaunt look that spoke of several long days spent on the trail.

"Howdy. You the law around here?" the stranger asked as he nodded at the badge pinned to Cody's shirt.

"I'm the deputy," Cody answered. "What can I do for you?"

"I'm looking for a man named Pierre Duquesne." The words were spoken without feeling, the tone flat, emotionless.

"You've got business with this fellow?" Cody asked bluntly.

A tiny smile played at the stranger's mouth. "I suppose you could say that," he replied. "If you're worried that I've come to cause trouble, Deputy, don't be. I'm not gunning for anybody."

"Fair enough," Cody said with a nod. Then he frowned. "Duquesne . . . the name's familiar, but I'm afraid I don't know where he lives." After a moment's pause, he went on, "I'll tell you what, let's go to the marshal's office and ask him. Marshal

Travis knows everybody in town. Do you have any objection to that?"

This time the stranger grinned broadly. "I'm not wanted, either," he said with a laugh. "I don't mind at all if we go to the marshal's office."

Feeling a little foolish, Cody returned the grin. The buckskinned man had seen right through him. *Well, I've never been known for my subtlety,* Cody thought. When it came to outlaws and pretty ladies —the two things that concerned him most—he usually followed a simple, direct course.

The stranger swung from his saddle and, leading the horse across the street, fell in step beside Cody. Despite the early hour, the sun was hot, and it felt good to step into the cool shade of the boardwalk's awning in front of the marshal's office. The stranger flipped his horse's reins over the hitchrack and followed the deputy into the simple plank building.

Marshal Luke Travis was sitting at his desk, scanning the local newspaper as he sipped a cup of coffee. When the two men walked in, he glanced up, and his keen eyes narrowed with interest at the man he did not know.

"Morning, Cody," Travis said to his deputy. As he nodded a greeting to the stranger, he unfolded his long legs and stood up.

The marshal was a handsome, broad-shouldered man with thick, sandy-brown hair that was a shade lighter than the full mustache that drooped over his wide mouth. Only the fine lines around his intelligent eyes and the glints of gray at his temples suggested that the youthful-looking marshal was on the far side of forty. On his lean frame he wore a brown work shirt and denim pants over comfortable boots. Both the holster and the Colt .44 slung at his hip had seen a lot of use.

Cody gestured to the stranger and said, "This man is looking for somebody named Pierre Duquesne, Marshal. Do you know the man?"

As Travis's eyes narrowed in thought, the stranger said, "Duquesne is older than I am, Marshal, around fifty. I don't know what he looks like now; it's been a long time since I've seen him."

Cody shot a glance at Travis. "That wouldn't be the fellow they call Frenchy, would it?"

"I think you're right, Cody," Travis said. "I believe I have heard him called Pierre." He looked at the stranger again. "You mind if I ask what you want with this man?"

The stranger grinned wearily. "Your deputy asked me the same thing, Marshal. I told him that I don't intend to start any trouble."

"I'm responsible for keeping the peace in Abilene," Travis said evenly. "Knowing who's liable to break it is part of the job."

The stranger drew a deep breath, and the pleasant expression vanished from his face. "My name is White Elk Duquesne," he said. "Pierre Duquesne is my father."

Both Travis and Cody were stunned. The marshal coughed and muttered, "I didn't know Duquesne had any grown kids."

The stranger frowned abruptly, as if puzzled by the remark. But instead of asking questions, he provided more information. "I have not seen my father in many years, Marshal. I simply want to say hello to him and be on my way."

Travis nodded. "I know where Fren—I mean, I know where your father lives. But I don't guarantee that he's there. He works as a driver for some of Abilene's freight companies, and he may be away on a run."

"I had heard that he had taken up freighting," White Elk said. "To be honest, Marshal, I was not sure if I would find him here. My father always moved around a great deal."

"I expect he's settled down since you've seen him," Travis said cryptically. He came from behind the desk and reached for a wide-brimmed, flat-crowned brown hat that hung on a peg just inside the door. "I'd be glad to take you to his house."

"Thanks, Marshal. I was hoping somebody might be able to tell me where to find him."

Travis led the two young men out of the office and turned east. White Elk stepped into the street, picked up his horse's reins, and fell in step beside the marshal and his deputy. Travis said, "Your father's place is on Third Street."

Cody stared at the marshal. Some of the finest homes in Abilene were on Third Street. J.G. McCoy, one of the founders of the town, still lived there. The deputy did not expect to find an itinerant freighter and former fur trapper living in a posh neighborhood like that. Travis evidently knew more about the man than he was saying.

As they walked along the street, Travis said, "I remember hearing about a scout named Duquesne who rode for General Mackenzie during the Red River War."

"That was me," White Elk said with a nod. "I'm

on the Army's books as a civilian Indian scout. My mother was a Kiowa squaw, so the officers in charge of the campaign chose me to help track down Quanah Parker and the big band he had gathered."

Neither lawman was surprised by White Elk's admission that he was a half-breed. His high cheekbones and dark skin spoke eloquently of his heritage. What was unusual, however, was that this half-breed had obviously spent a great deal of time in the white man's world and had had some education.

"I've heard about Quanah Parker," Cody said with growing interest. "He gave the Army quite a fight down in Texas."

White Elk nodded. "Quanah managed to do something few chiefs have done. He not only led his own people, the Quahadi Comanche, into the battle, but he persuaded the Kiowa and the Cheyenne to join them. For a time, the Texas frontier was no place for a white man." The buckskinned man's voice grew solemn as he went on, "All that's over now. Mackenzie tracked them to Palo Duro Canyon and defeated the Indians on their own ground. Most of the warriors are on reservations now."

"You sound like you think that might not be a good thing," Cody commented.

White Elk smiled and shrugged his shoulders. "I am half Kiowa, Deputy. There's a part of me that regrets what has happened to them. They are a proud people. I should know, I lived with them for many years when I was a child."

"Your father stayed with the tribe?" Travis asked.

White Elk shook his head. "No. My father left when I was a baby. I did not see him again until after my mother died." There was a touch of bitterness in his reply.

Travis and Cody could understand the man's feelings. Both of them had seen how half-breeds were reviled by white men and red men alike, unwelcome in either world.

Even now, quite a few people stared as White Elk Duquesne passed them on the street. While many of Abilene's townfolk had lived on the frontier for years and were accustomed to buckskins, others had only recently arrived from the East. To them, White Elk probably looked like something out of a dime novel with his broad-brimmed hat, fringed costume, bowie knife, and long-barreled pistol.

The scout was aware of the stares, too. Cody could tell that from the way he glanced around quickly. Yet White Elk had to be comfortable to speak of his background so readily.

"My grandfather was a mountain man," the scout went on. "Henri Duquesne was his name, and he traveled in the Rockies with Jim Bridger and Jim Beckwourth and the others. He probably had Indian wives, too, but he always came back to my grandmother Josette in Illinois. My father followed in his father's footsteps, coming south to follow the Santa Fe Trail. He met my mother somewhere along the way, spent a year with her and her people, and then moved on. As I was growing up, I knew my father was a white man, but it didn't make any difference to me. It did to my mother's people, though."

The three men had been walking north on Buckeye Street, and now Travis turned east on Third at the intersection.

"It must have been hard on you, growing up in an Indian camp with a long-gone white father," Travis said sympathetically.

White Elk laughed shortly. "I've never wasted any time pitying myself, Marshal. No need for you to, either. When I was a boy, I learned how to ride, shoot, hunt, and take care of myself. I always seemed to have what I needed to get along in life. How other folks felt about me didn't matter."

"That's a good way to look at it," Travis replied. He had seen many half-breeds who had not coped so well with their mixed-blood heritage and had turned to lives of crime.

"When my mother died, I figured the time had come for me to leave the Kiowas," White Elk went on. "I was only fourteen winters at the time, but the way I saw it, I was a man. My mother had told me that when my father left, he was heading for New Mexico, so I started for there myself. I finally found him in Taos." He chuckled humorlessly. "He had taken up with a Hopi woman and wasn't too happy to find a skinny half-Kiowa whelp on his doorstep."

"I've never met Duquesne," Travis said dryly, "but I can imagine."

"We stayed together for a while," White Elk went on. "But there were too many grudges on both sides. We couldn't get along. I thought it would be better for me to try to make my own way in the world. I wound up working for the Army, been doing that ever since."

"What made you decide to come to Abilene?" Travis asked. He knew he was prying, but White Elk did not seem to mind.

"I had some time coming to me," the half-breed answered. "Thought it might be a good idea to look up my father and see how he's doing. I don't like having unfinished business, Marshal."

The three men had passed the McCoy house. The homes along Third Street were substantial, some made of stone, others of whitewashed clapboard. All were well maintained and neat, as were the yards that surrounded them. Spring had been warm and wet, and the trees and grass were a lush green. Carefully tended flower beds were beginning to bloom.

Travis paused in front of a freshly whitewashed frame house. The rather small yard, which was attractively enclosed by a white picket fence, was as carefully maintained as the other plots on the street. Brightly colored flowers had been planted in front of the porch, and a bench swing hung from its roof. It was a very pleasant house, the kind of place that was definitely a home.

"This is it," Travis said. "If we're thinking about the same Duquesne, then this is where your father lives."

White Elk stared at the house and shook his head. "This is a far cry from some of the other places he's lived in," he whispered in astonishment. "Compared to the hovel where he was staying in New Mexico, this is a palace."

"He must've come up in the world since then," Cody said. "I've got to admit—" The marshal glared at him, and Cody abruptly stopped speaking.

Travis looked at White Elk and inclined his head

toward the house. "If you really want to see your father, don't you think you'd better go up and knock on the door?" he asked.

"I do," White Elk nodded. A look of apprehension passed over his features. As a scout for the Army, he must have faced all sorts of dangers, but this challenge obviously unnerved him.

He pushed open the gate in the picket fence and strode up the smooth stone walk. Travis and Cody did not follow but stood watching outside the fence until White Elk stepped onto the porch. With a sigh, the marshal started to turn away. "Come on, Cody. The man's got a right to a private reunion."

Cody nodded. "That's true. I'm really surprised to see that Frenchy Duquesne lives in a house like this. I usually see him in the rougher places in town."

Travis glanced over his shoulder and saw White Elk Duquesne lifting his hand to knock on the door. "You're not as surprised as that fellow will be in a minute or so," he said dryly.

Chapter Two

WHITE ELK'S STOMACH KNOTTED PAINFULLY AS HE waited for someone to answer his knock. He did not know why he was so nervous. He had thought long and hard before he set out to find his father, and he had made the trip to Abilene certain that it was what he wanted to do. But deciding on a course of action and then seeing it through were often two different things.

He had never regretted leaving his father and finding his own way in the world. As time passed he had become convinced that he had done the right thing, and he had made a good life for himself. There was danger in it, of course, and loneliness, but those were things that White Elk could tolerate. He was his own man.

Nevertheless, the memory of the angry parting

between father and son had haunted him. Pierre Duquesne was not an endearing man, not someone easy to love, but he was White Elk's only blood relative. White Elk believed deeply that it was wrong that they should remember each other badly.

The quick patter of footsteps beyond the door startled him. The knob turned, and the door swung open. A woman's voice said, "Yes? Who is—"

She gasped and stopped speaking, obviously shocked by the sight of this tall, buckskin-clad stranger on her porch.

White Elk was stunned. He had one overwhelming impression: She was beautiful. He stared silently into her china-blue eyes and, after a long moment, shifted his gaze. She was a young woman in her early twenties. Fine, long, cornsilk-blond hair framed her lovely face. She was clad in a light blue dress, the fabric dotted with tiny white flowers, and he was surprised further when he noticed that her belly was swollen with impending motherhood. Her pregnancy only enhanced her beauty, for her skin was luminous, and her eyes were clear and sparkling. As she stood in the doorway, the picture she made was one of the most compelling White Elk had ever seen.

Recovering his composure, he reached up and snatched off his hat. He nodded jerkily and said, "Ma'am."

The young woman replied. "Hello. What can I do for you, sir?"

"Is this . . . is this the house of Pierre Duquesne, ma'am?"

"It is," she said.

"Would it be too much for me to ask if he is here?"

The woman shook her head. "It would not be too much to ask, sir. Unfortunately, Pierre isn't at home at the moment. Perhaps I might be able to help you. I'm Mrs. Duquesne."

White Elk had half expected her to say that, but hearing the words spoken still came as a shock. This woman—his stepmother—was even younger than he was.

Should I tell her who I am? The question raced through his mind. After a second or two, he decided not to, at least not yet. Instead he said, "Do you know when he'll be back?"

"Why, I expect him sometime this morning. He's a freighter, you know—" She paused and waited for White Elk to nod in confirmation, then went on, "He'll be returning from a short run he made to Solomon yesterday. It's only a few miles, so he should be back before noon."

White Elk sighed. Clearly, this woman had never lived on the frontier. Out on the fringes of civilization a woman did not admit that she was alone. If she did, she had better have the sense to say that her man would be returning any minute. With some of the men who roamed the wilds, to do otherwise was to invite disaster.

"Excuse me, ma'am," he began gently. "It isn't wise to tell a stranger that your husband won't be back for a while."

She frowned. "But you just asked me when Pierre would be home."

"I know, and I thank you for the honest answer."

White Elk glanced around at the tranquil neighborhood and shook his head. "I've just been on the trail too long, ma'am. You're right, of course."

He had recovered from his initial shock, but nervousness threatened to overwhelm him once more. As the unusual feeling of panic rose in his chest, he decided it would be best if he came back later. He started to turn away.

"Just a moment," the woman said, stopping him. "You didn't tell me why you want to see Pierre."

Abruptly, White Elk swung around and faced her. "I'm sorry, ma'am. It's personal. I'll drop by later, when your husband is home," he said quickly.

He backed toward the edge of the porch. To his surprise, the woman followed him with a strange expression on her face. Suddenly her eyes lit up, and she reached out and touched his arm.

"I know you!" she exclaimed. "You looked so familiar when I first saw you, and now I know why. It's the resemblance to Pierre. You're White Elk!"

"You . . . know about me?" he stammered.

"Of course. Pierre told me." Grasping his sleeve, she started to pull him gently toward the door. "Come in, please. We have so much to talk about, and I'm sure Pierre will be thrilled to see you."

White Elk was not so certain of that, but he permitted the woman to steer him into the cool, shadowy interior of the house. As they stepped into the foyer, he saw a table with a beautifully carved base standing against one wall. The highly polished tabletop gleamed, and an elaborately crocheted doily decorated it. Hanging on the wall above the table was a chromolithograph of a woodland scene. Behind the door, he glimpsed a hall tree.

The woman held his arm as they stepped into a parlor that opened to the left. A rug was centered on the polished hardwood floor. A long divan was on the far side of the room with a low table in front of it. At the end of the divan another table held a kerosene lamp. Two upholstered chairs stood opposite the divan, and against the far wall was a pianoforte. Several pastoral pictures and two shelves filled with knickknacks decorated the walls.

It was a pleasant, comfortable room, but White Elk felt stifled. He was accustomed to open spaces. Even on the rare occasions when he slept indoors, it was in a barracks or some bawdy house—not like this at all.

"Where are my manners?" the woman asked as she guided him toward the divan. "My name is Lora, Lora Duquesne. And you're White Elk, of course. Would you like some coffee?"

"Ah . . . yes. That would be nice."

"I have a pot on the stove. I'll be right back. Please, sit down."

As she bustled from the room, White Elk saw that the advanced stage of her pregnancy did not keep her from being active. He sighed deeply and took a seat. Glancing down, he noticed his grimy, dust-covered buckskins, sat up abruptly, and perched like a nervous schoolboy on the very edge of the divan. He did not want to soil this lady's furniture.

Slowly he studied the room in the filtered daylight that came through curtained windows. It was undeniably a woman's room. He could see no sign that his father spent much time here.

The old man must have spent some time in another room of the house, though, White Elk thought with a grin. Lora Duquesne's condition was proof of that. Unless—

He shook his head—*that* was a totally unwarranted conclusion. He had just met Lora and had no reason to suspect her of being unfaithful to his father. Maybe Pierre *had* changed over the years. There had to have been some reason for a fine lady like Lora to marry him.

Tinkling china announced Lora's passage down the hallway, and she came into the room carrying a silver tray that held a coffeepot and two cups. Setting the tray on the low table in front of the divan, she smiled as she sat down in one of the upholstered chairs. White Elk noticed that a row of delicate flowers was painted around the bases of the cups. That feminine touch was another surprise.

He had not expected to find that his father was married. Living with some worn-out soiled dove perhaps, but not married to a fresh young thing like Lora.

She poured coffee for both of them and handed him a cup. As he took it, her fingertips brushed his. "I hope you like your coffee black," she said. "That's the way Pierre takes his, and I thought with you being his son and all . . ."

"This is fine," he assured her. He sipped the hot liquid. "Very good, in fact."

She tasted her own coffee, then said with a smile, "Now, you have to tell me all about yourself, White Elk. I've always hoped that I would meet you."

He placed his cup on the tray and took a deep breath. "I'm surprised Pierre even mentioned me," he said bluntly. "Most men wouldn't talk about a half-breed son that they fathered by some Kiowa squaw."

Lora blanched at the harsh words, and he instantly regretted them. He did not mean to hurt her, but he felt too uncomfortable to worry about being diplomatic.

"Pierre told me everything about his life before he met me, White Elk," she said with a smile. "I know about your mother and you. When two people are in love, they owe it to each other to have no secrets. I told Pierre everything about my own past, too."

He could not stop himself from grinning. Given her age and the air of innocence she exuded, she could not have had much to confess. "I'd wager the old man's yarn was a little more colorful," he said. "No offense, Lora."

"Of course not. At any rate, I always thought it was a shame that you and Pierre parted on such bad terms. I told him several times that he ought to get in touch with you. After all, we knew where you were."

"Knew where I was?" White Elk exclaimed. "How?"

"Oh, since Pierre is in the freight business, he talks to people from all over. He heard quite a few stories about that dashing Army scout, White Elk Duquesne. Now that you're here, I can see that you really are as dashing as the stories made you out to be."

"I'm not sure about that," he commented dryly.

"The truth sometimes gets lost in the tales that people tell."

She reached out, took his hand, and squeezed it. "Well, I'm glad you're here. I'm sure that Pierre will be thrilled to see you."

He could not reply to that. He did not share Lora's certainty that his father would welcome him.

He looked at her smiling, dimpled face for a long moment—long enough that she looked away and blushed. He said, "How in the world did my father capture a lovely young woman like you?"

"I'm not that lovely," she said, still not meeting his eyes. "I'm so big right now, I don't know what Pierre must think of me."

"If he has any sense, he thinks you're beautiful," White Elk said.

She brushed aside the compliment with a wave of her hand. "My father owns a store in Junction City," she said. "Pierre used to deliver merchandise. I worked in the store from the time I was a little girl, and that's how we met. Pierre was always friendly to me. He used to say that I should be wearing fine, fancy clothes, instead of selling them."

"Well, he was right about that," White Elk said.

"I . . . I have to admit that when he started courting me, I was quite taken aback. I never thought that an older man would be interested in someone like me. I suppose you could say Pierre swept me off my feet. He was so charming, such a gentleman."

That did not sound at all like the father he remembered, White Elk thought. People could change, but there was something peculiar about this situation. His instincts told him there was more to the story than Lora was telling. Perhaps even more than she knew.

"He bought this house for me," Lora continued. "He told me to fix it up in any way that I liked. Money was no object. That was a little over a year ago. I've tried to make him proud of me and of our home."

"I'm sure he is," White Elk said. "Only a fool wouldn't be. And my father, despite his rough edges, was never a fool."

"Oh, no. He's made me very happy."

Lora was undoubtedly sincere. White Elk had never heard a woman sound so in love and convinced that her husband loved her in return. As he looked at her shining face, he wished for her sake that he could shake the uneasy feeling that was nagging at him.

They had been talking for quite a while. White Elk sipped the now cool coffee and then said, "Since you don't know exactly when my father will be back, it might be better for me to go now. I can always come back later. . . ."

"I won't hear of it," Lora declared firmly. "I want you to wait right here for him. You can have lunch with us, and I want you to stay with us. We have a spare bedroom." She blushed. "It's been turned into a nursery, but the bed is still in there, and we can push the cradle against the wall."

The prospect of spending the night in the room intended for his future half brother or half sister only increased White Elk's uneasiness. He replaced the cup on the tray, put his hands on his knees, and stood up. "I don't want to put anybody out . . ." he began.

"Nonsense!" Lora exclaimed, as she, too, rose. Suddenly she cocked her head, as if she were listening to some sound outside. "Besides," she said with a bright smile, "I think I hear Pierre coming now."

White Elk had noticed nothing, but now that she mentioned it, he heard the front gate squeak as it was closed. Footsteps crunched on the stone walk and clumped on the wooden porch. As White Elk and Lora turned toward the foyer, the front door opened.

A man nearly as tall as White Elk strode into the house. The resemblance between father and son was striking. Pierre Duquesne was naturally lean and wiry, and a lifetime of hard work had enhanced those qualities. He wore work boots, corduroy pants, and a tan shirt. Beneath a battered black hat that was shoved back on his head was a thick, curly mass of iron-gray hair. His face was lined and weathered, and he turned shocked eyes toward his wife and their visitor.

"Look who's here, Pierre!" Lora exclaimed enthusiastically. "It's White Elk."

Pierre stood silently in the foyer for only a moment, but it seemed like an hour to White Elk. Then, slowly, he nodded and said, "I can see that, Lora. What's he doing here?" Despite his name, his speech was unaccented. Long years away from his French-speaking parents had erased any accent he had had.

For an instant Lora looked stricken by the blunt words. But she quickly recovered her enthusiastic expression and continued brightly, "He's come to pay us a visit, Pierre. Isn't that wonderful? After all these years, your son has come to see you just as you're about to be blessed with another child." She gently patted her stomach.

Pierre took off his hat and hung it on the hall tree. As he stepped into the parlor, he narrowed his eyes and regarded White Elk suspiciously. Nodding curtly, he said, "How are you, boy?"

"I'm fine, Pa," White Elk replied, wondering if he should offer to shake hands with this man who was little more than a stranger to him. He decided against the gesture. From the look in Pierre's eyes, it would not mean much.

"What are you doing here?"

"I came to see you," White Elk answered honestly. He glanced quickly at Lora, who was watching the reunion and trying not to look too anxious. "I thought it was time we made peace between us."

"Fine," Pierre grunted. "I hold no grudges. That take care of it?"

White Elk felt anger building in him. Nothing had changed. All his father had to do was step into the same room with him, and they were instantly at each other's throats.

"It was a mistake," the scout said. "Just a mistake." He looked at Lora again and forced a smile. "I'm sorry, ma'am. I'd better be going."

Lowering his head, he started toward the foyer and stepped around Pierre.

"Please wait!" Lora said sharply. As he glanced over his shoulder at her, she went on in a softer tone, "Please, White Elk, don't leave yet."

"The boy said he has to go," Pierre said gruffly.

"I think we should let him do what he wants, Lora."

Acting on a sudden perverse impulse, White Elk said, "All right, Mrs. Duquesne. I'll wait."

"Thank you. And I told you my name is Lora." White Elk saw that she looked more in command of herself as she turned to face her husband. "I don't know what's wrong, Pierre, but you're not acting like yourself at all. White Elk is your son, and he's come a long way to see you. You have come a long way, haven't you, White Elk?"

"All the way from Indian Territory," he replied. He was beginning to enjoy the uncomfortable expression that was appearing on his father's face. Beneath Lora's softness and beauty was a well of strength and determination that White Elk was just beginning to appreciate.

"Figures," Pierre snapped. "That's where all the Kiowas are these days. I supposed you had taken up with some squaw down there."

"Like you did?" White Elk shot back.

Lora insinuated herself between them. "Please, I don't want you two to argue. This should be a happy occasion. Please, Pierre. I know you're really happy to see your son. You just don't want to admit it."

Pierre took a deep breath. He hesitated, then stuck out a calloused hand to White Elk. "All right, dammit," he muttered. "Glad to see you, boy. You been doing all right?"

White Elk took his hand and returned the firm grip. "I'm fine," he said, still relishing the uncomfortable look in his father's eyes. His own nervousness had eased somewhat now that Lora was taking his side. He could tell that she intended to make this meeting a friendly one, by herself if she had to.

"Still working for the Army?" Pierre asked.

White Elk nodded. "I had some time off coming to me, so I decided to look you up. Never expected to find that you were about to become a daddy again."

"That's enough about that!" Pierre said sharply. "It's none of your business, boy."

White Elk held up his hands, palms out, and grinned. "Whatever you say, Pa. Whether you believe it or not, I am glad to see you. You look like the freight business has been good to you."

"We're getting by," Pierre replied curtly.

"Of course we are," Lora said. "We're getting along just fine." She slid smoothly between the two men and linked arms with each of them. As she spoke, she guided them toward the divan. "Now, I want you both to come over here and sit down. You can have a nice long talk while I start lunch. White Elk, you will stay, won't you?"

"I'd be honored, Lora." He nodded as he sat on the divan next to his father.

"And you'll let us put you up while you're here?"

He saw that she was a very determined young woman and would not let that one go. As uncomfortable as the idea made him, he did not want to argue with her. "That would be just fine," he said.

"Wonderful." She smiled brightly, obviously pleased by her efforts. Then she moved to the door of the parlor and paused to look back at the two stiff figures. "I'm so glad you came. I'm sure you'll have a fine visit."

White Elk and Pierre exchanged a doubtful

glance and sat in silence until Lora had disappeared down the hall into the kitchen. When her footsteps died away, Pierre looked over at him and said, "You can just forget about staying here, boy. There's no room, no matter what Lora says."

"It was not my idea," White Elk replied stiffly. "I just didn't want to offend her."

"I'll take care of that. You don't have to worry about hurting her feelings. She's my wife, and she'll do as I say."

White Elk grinned humorlessly. "I see you haven't changed much."

"Neither have you," Pierre snapped back and glared at him. "You always were an uppity young pup."

White Elk leaned forward and looked at his father with an earnest, serious expression. "Look, Pa, I know I made a mistake coming here. You don't want me around, and to be honest, I don't want to be here anymore. Maybe I'd best go while your wife's busy." He started to get up.

Pierre frowned and reached out, as if to touch White Elk, but he stopped himself. "Don't be so damned hotheaded, boy," he growled. "I don't want Lora getting all upset, not in her condition. Just sit back down."

White Elk was startled by the concern in his father's voice. Evidently Pierre was genuinely fond of Lora. The man White Elk knew as his father would have married her simply to enjoy her young, supple body in bed for a while. Once he tired of her or she became pregnant, the old Pierre would have left, heedless of any hurt he would cause. But this

Pierre clearly intended to be a husband to this young woman and a father to their child.

Taking a deep breath, Pierre went on, "You just shocked me by showing up like this, son. I didn't expect to ever see you again."

"Lora said you told her about . . . my mother and me."

Pierre nodded. "She wanted to know about my past, and I figured she had a right to hear about it, so she'd know what she was getting if she married me. She's never held anything against me, boy. She's more forgiving than some folks."

Ignoring the implications in the comment, White Elk said, "I'll stay for lunch, to please Lora. But I do think it'd be best if I slept someplace else tonight."

"How long are you planning to stay in Abilene?" Pierre asked.

White Elk shrugged. "I haven't given it much thought. I've got a couple of weeks left before I have to get back to the Army. I am still a civilian. I wouldn't even have to go back if I decided not to." He grinned again; this time the expression contained some genuine humor. "I could even stay right here in Abilene if I wanted to."

Pierre frowned nervously. "You wouldn't do that, would you?"

The scout laughed. "I doubt that I could stand staying in a town for too long. I imagine I'll be on my way again in a day or two."

"In that case, I know where you can stay." Pierre lowered his voice as he went on, "Go see a lady named Grace Pinkston. She runs a boardinghouse on Walnut Street. Any man in town can tell you where to find it. Tell Grace I sent you."

White Elk nodded. "I'll do that." He wondered why his father had spoken so quietly and was about to question him when Lora appeared in the parlor doorway.

She wore a crisp white apron now, and her flushed face indicated that she had been working hard at the stove. Delicious aromas wafted from the kitchen behind her. She smiled at the two men sitting on the divan.

"You two are getting along just fine now, aren't you?" she asked brightly.

"Sure," White Elk replied.

"I knew you would," Lora declared. "The bond between father and son cannot be broken easily."

White Elk glanced at Pierre. While the older man's lined face wore a pleasant expression, his eyes were icily cold.

Let Lora believe what she wants, White Elk decided. For now, that was enough.

Chapter Three

———◆———

THE LUNCH THAT LORA HAD PREPARED WAS A FAR CRY
from the grub in the Army mess halls or the simple
fare that White Elk carried on the trail. Lora had
spread a crisp, white linen cloth on the dining room
table and set fragrant platters of ham, sweet potatoes, beans, greens, and flaky biscuits upon it.
White Elk enjoyed the meal more than any he had
had in months.

Of course, it would have been even more enjoy-
able if Pierre had not sat stiffly at the head of the
table, shoveling food into his mouth and speaking
only in grunts and monosyllables. Lora had to
carry the conversation almost by herself.

She did a good job of it, White Elk had to admit.
She was as bright and cheerful as a spring sunrise,
and she kept the atmosphere around the table light

and friendly. Question after question about his life as an Army scout tumbled from her mouth, and White Elk tried to answer all of them. Glossing over the more unpleasant aspects, he concentrated instead on relating anecdotes about the famous soldiers with whom he had served. Inevitably, Lora asked about the most famous of them all.

"I knew Custer," White Elk answered solemnly. "Never rode with the Seventh Cavalry, though. I've been attached to Mackenzie and the Fourth most of the time. The Fourth has a great record and has fought in plenty of battles, but we never ran into anything like Yellowhair did on the Little Big-horn."

"Yellowhair?" Lora frowned.

"That's what the Indians called Custer," White Elk explained. "They didn't respect him very much, despite what you may have read in the newspapers. To tell you the truth, neither did I. He seemed to think he was immortal." The scout shook his head. "He learned differently."

"The man was doing his job," Pierre said.

"Maybe," White Elk said with a nod. "At least, that was the way he saw it."

"It was a horrible thing," Lora said with a shudder. "I don't think I want to talk about it."

"It won't happen again," White Elk assured her. "Any officer who felt the way Custer did has learned his lesson. The Indians are losing the war anyway. Without the buffalo, they can't last. And so many of the buffalo are gone now. . . ."

White Elk's voice trailed off as sad images filtered into his thoughts. With hordes of railroad workers swarming across the frontier, hunters had drastically thinned the vast buffalo herds to provide food for the workers. Then, after the completion of the railroad, the demand for buffalo hides had brought on an even greater slaughter. In Dodge City he had seen piles of hides that were as tall as buildings. Driven south by the persistent hunters, the buffalo herds that had once numbered in the millions had dwindled dramatically. With the shaggy beasts had gone a way of life that had supported the Indians for centuries.

"No great loss," Pierre said. "I've got nothing against Indians—"

White Elk barely suppressed his surging anger. *That's awfully big of you, Pierre,* the scout thought, *considering that you had a squaw and a half-breed son.*

"But the Army is going to have to pacify them if the West is ever going to be settled. We haven't had any Indian trouble around here for a long time, and you can see how Abilene has grown. Folks don't want to live where they may be scalped at any time."

White Elk considered his father's unusually long speech for a moment, then said, "I can't say that I disagree with you. After all, I work for the Army. But from what I've seen, the white men have brought a lot of their troubles on themselves."

Pierre scowled. "I should have expected as much—"

"Is this your first visit to Abilene, White Elk?" Lora interrupted quickly.

He nodded. "I've been to Dodge and Wichita

before, but this is the first time I've come to this part of the state. It looks like good country. I rode past some fine-looking ranches and farms."

"It is quite a fertile land," Lora said. She glanced down at her stomach, then flushed at the possible double meaning of her words.

"I've been thinking," Pierre said. "I don't know that it would be fitting for you to stay here with Lora being so close to her time."

"I agree," White Elk said quickly, before Lora could object. The last thing he wanted to do was spend a night under the same roof as Pierre Duquesne. For one of the rare times in his life, he and his father agreed about something. "I don't want to be a burden," he said, smiling at Lora, "under the circumstances."

"But you wouldn't be any burden," Lora protested.

"It's all right," White Elk said soothingly. "I'd feel better if you'd let me find another place to stay." He did not mention his father's recommendation of Grace Pinkston's boardinghouse.

"Well . . . of course you're free to do as you please." Lora was silent for a moment and then brightened as an idea struck her. "That would be fine, White Elk. As long as you spend some more time with us while you're in Abilene."

"I will," he promised, not looking at Pierre.

Little more was said while the three of them finished their lunch. When he pushed his chair away from the table, White Elk was pleasantly full. "That meal was worth every mile I spent on the trail, ma'am," he said sincerely.

"Thank you," Lora responded. "I'm glad you enjoyed it."

"Be glad to help you clean up," he offered.

"No, indeed," Lora replied as she stood up. "I'm still quite capable of handling my responsibilities."

White Elk noticed that Pierre did not offer to help. Instead, the freighter stood up and took a cigar from his shirt pocket. He lit it but did not offer one to White Elk.

The scout had stood up when Lora did, and now as she started to carry one of the platters to the kitchen, he said, "I'd best be going. I have to find a room. I don't imagine that will be much of a problem."

"There's always the Drovers' Cottage," Lora said, naming the well-known hotel where many cowboys driving herds from Texas had stayed over the years. "And the Grand Palace on Texas Street—" Abruptly she stopped speaking and flushed.

As he chewed on his cigar, Pierre said, "Lora just realized that neither of those places will take redskins."

"Don't worry," White Elk said coolly. "I'm sure I'll easily find a place."

He wondered briefly if he would encounter that prejudice at Grace Pinkston's. Would Pierre send him to an establishment knowing that he would be turned down? White Elk could not be certain.

Lora had taken his hat earlier and placed it on the hall tree in the foyer. As White Elk went to it now, Pierre sauntered after him. Lora hurriedly carried another platter into the kitchen, then bustled down the hall toward them, wiping her hands on her white apron.

"I'm so glad you came," she told White Elk as she paused beside Pierre. "Will you be back for supper tonight?"

"We'll see," White Elk replied. "I think there's a good chance I'll be busy."

"Oh. Well, please feel free to stop by anytime you want. You're always welcome in our home. Isn't he, Pierre?"

"Sure," Pierre said shortly, exhaling a cloud of acrid smoke. "Anytime."

White Elk heard the insincerity in his father's voice and knew that Pierre was only saying it to keep Lora happy. *At least he's willing to make an effort,* White Elk thought. He still disliked his father intensely, but he had to admit that Pierre had changed. The old Pierre Duquesne would not have cared about Lora's happiness.

The scout put his hand on the doorknob, ready to turn it and step out. Lora placed a hand on White Elk's arm and, rising up on tiptoes, planted a light, stepmotherly kiss on his lean cheek. White Elk smiled and noticed a disapproving frown flash across Pierre's face. *Good,* he thought. *Let the old scoundrel be annoyed.*

"Good-bye," he said softly.

"Good-bye," Lora echoed.

He untied his horse, mounted up, and headed toward downtown Abilene, convinced that he would have no trouble finding someone who would direct him to Grace Pinkston's boardinghouse on Walnut Street.

As he rode, he reflected on the hours he had just spent in his father's house. The time had been a mixture of anger, awkwardness, and some genuine pleasure. The best part of the day had been when Lora was there. White Elk realized he already liked his stepmother. He had never expected to encounter a stepmother—especially not one as young and pretty as Lora—but he had enjoyed her company. He could still feel the warmth of her lips on his cheek. . . .

He shook his head. Despite her age, she *was* his father's pregnant wife. He had no business being attracted to her, no matter how beautiful she was. No matter how fine and soft her hair had been when it lightly brushed his cheek—

With an effort, he willed those thoughts away and concentrated on finding Grace Pinkston's place.

When he reached Texas Street, White Elk stopped in front of a large general mercantile. The ornately painted sign that hung in the window read THE GREAT WESTERN STORE. A steady stream of townspeople moved through its double doors, and shop clerks were busily loading sacks of supplies into two of the many wagons parked in front of it.

White Elk urged his horse closer to one of the wagons and nodded to the clerk who was tossing a sack of flour into the wagon bed. "Howdy," he said. "Pretty day, isn't it?"

The clerk barely glanced at him. "Guess it is if you don't have to work," he responded.

"Mind telling me where I might find Walnut Street?"

"Two blocks west," the aproned clerk said.

"You know of a boardinghouse run by a lady named Grace Pinkston?"

Abruptly, the man looked up and scrutinized White Elk closely. He frowned. "I'm not sure it's the place you're lookin' for, mister, but you might check at the house on the corner at Walnut and Fourth. Big place, you can't miss it."

White Elk nodded again. "Thanks, friend." He heeled his horse into motion.

"Hey, mister!" the clerk called after him. White Elk turned and looked over his shoulder. "You a half-breed?"

"What of it?" White Elk asked tightly.

The clerk held up his hands, palms out. "No offense, mister. I just thought I'd warn you not to get your hopes up."

White Elk stared coldly at the man for a long moment, then rode on. As he followed the clerk's directions he realized that he need not have gone all the way to Texas Street; there was a much shorter route from Pierre's house. Without a doubt, Pierre could have told him, but his father had never gone out of his way to help anyone. In fact, Pierre had usually done everything possible to make things more difficult, as if watching his son struggle gave him some sort of perverse pleasure.

The clerk was right—it would have been hard to miss the big house. The sprawling, two-story stone structure stood on a sweeping, tree-shaded lawn. A driveway led to a large stable located behind the house that was partly visible from the street.

White Elk tied his mount to one of the two hitchracks in front of the house next to a couple of other horses. He glanced at the stable and noticed that a pair of buggies were parked there. Some of the boarders appeared to be home, even though it was early afternoon, when most folks were still working.

A pebbled walk curved under the trees to the porch of the house. As White Elk started up it, his scout's instincts told him someone was watching him. He noticed a curtain flutter at one of the long, narrow windows to the left of the front door. Someone had been peeking around them.

He stepped onto the porch and paused before lifting the brass lion's-head knocker on the thick, ornately carved door. Most boardinghouses in which he had stayed had been rough clapboard affairs, not solid structures like this one. He wondered how much room and board Grace Pinkston had to charge to maintain a place like this.

White Elk rapped sharply with the knocker, then waited. A moment later, the door opened slightly, and a middle-aged woman peered at him through the crack. White Elk nodded and touched the brim of his hat. "Would you be Mrs. Pinkston, ma'am?" he asked.

"Yes, I'm Grace Pinkston," the woman answered in a husky voice. Dark hair touched with gray was smoothed back from a strong-featured, handsome face. The dress she wore was the same deep shade of blue as her intense, assessing eyes.

"I was sent here—" White Elk began.

"One moment, young man," Grace Pinkston said abruptly as she scrutinized him. "You have some Indian blood in you."

White Elk's jaw tightened. "I'm a half-breed," he

said curtly. "At least that's what some people call me."

Grace Pinkston started to close the door. "I'm sorry," she said with an icy politeness. "I'm afraid I can't take Indian customers. It would cause too many problems with the regulars."

White Elk had encountered that reaction often enough over the years that he should have handled it smoothly. But this was one of the rare times when his anger got the better of him. He slammed his hand against the door to prevent it from closing further and scowled at the woman. Grace Pinkston gasped and then glared angrily at him.

"Pierre Duquesne sent me here," White Elk said gruffly. "Does that name mean anything to you?"

At the mention of Pierre's name, Grace Pinkston's eyes narrowed in a puzzled frown. "Pierre told you to come here?" she asked. "What are you to him?"

That was none of the woman's business, White Elk thought, but he knew if he wanted to stay here, he would have to answer the question. "Duquesne is my father," he declared. "My name is White Elk Duquesne."

"Well, why didn't you say so in the first place?" she said with a broad smile. "Please, come in."

She stepped back and opened the door wide. White Elk hesitated for a moment, wondering why she had changed her mind so quickly. Then he shrugged and entered the house.

He could see now that Grace Pinkston had a fine figure for a woman of her age. The years had thickened her somewhat through the middle, but the impressive thrust of her bosom and the lush swell of her hips more than made up for that. She closed the door behind him and then, in a gesture of familiarity that took him by surprise, slid an arm through his.

"I can see the resemblance now," she said as she looked at him appraisingly. "You favor Pierre quite a bit. I'm sure that when he was your age he was every bit as handsome and dashing as you are, White Elk."

Flattered, he grinned. This was the second time today a lady had referred to him as dashing. He had never thought of himself that way.

He looked around the shadowy foyer. A thick, richly colored rug lay on the polished wood floor. The walls were paneled with dark wood. Across the foyer, a broad staircase wound upstairs; beside it, a long hall led to the rear of the house. Glancing to his right, he noticed a small sitting room furnished with a sofa and several armchairs that at the moment was deserted. Grace steered White Elk to his left, through an arched doorway into a large parlor. The parlor was anything but deserted, and White Elk was shocked by what he saw.

Four beautiful young women were lounging there. The heavy curtains over the windows were closed, blocking most of the sunlight. A pair of crystal chandeliers complete with a score of candles lit the room. In that soft, warm light the women's skin seemed to glow.

And there was plenty of exposed skin to reflect that light. All of the women were scantily clad. A short, lush brunette wore a black corset and step-ins that left her breasts and legs exposed. As she half-reclined on a divan, she smiled shamelessly at White Elk. Sitting at the other end of the divan was a slender young woman with waist-length raven black hair draped over her shoulders. The sweep of hair seemed to cover more of her slender body than did her sheer camisole. In a chair on the other side of the room sat a mulatto, her burnished skin a compelling contrast to the white gown she wore.

That left the young woman who was standing beside one of the windows. White Elk realized that that was the window where he had seen the curtains move. Had it been this woman who had flicked back those heavy velvet draperies to study him? If so, he boldly returned the favor.

Strawberry-blond hair fell in thick waves to her shoulders, framing a face that was undeniably beautiful. An insolent smile played on her full red lips, and her smoldering eyes were a deep green. The silk chemise that clung to every curve on her body was the same shade as her eyes. White Elk could not help notice her hard nipples straining against the delicate fabric.

This is no simple boardinghouse, White Elk thought. From the appearance of the women and the richly appointed furnishings, it was obvious that Grace Pinkston ran a highly successful bordello, and his father had sent him here. The old reprobate had not changed as much as he had first thought.

White Elk threw his head back and laughed. The absurdity of the situation kept him laughing for a full minute. Grace and her girls simply smiled at him, undoubtedly accustomed to some bizarre behavior from their customers.

When White Elk finally stopped laughing, he grinned at Grace and said, "Old Pierre must be quite a customer. I imagine he's keeping you pretty busy, what with his wife about to give birth."

The smile vanished from Grace's face. "You shouldn't say such things about your father," she chided him. "A son should be respectful."

"And a father should earn that respect," White Elk replied, his voice sharper than he had intended. He shook his head. "I didn't come here to argue, Mrs. Pinkston. Obviously my father was playing a joke on me. He told me I could rent a room here while I stayed in Abilene. I imagine the bill would add up pretty rapidly at hourly rates."

"You jump to too many conclusions, young man." Grace's eyes were stern.

"You mean I can rent a room here . . . for *sleeping?*"

"We'll talk about that later." Grace smiled in her practiced, professional way and took White Elk's arm again. He allowed her to turn him toward the languid young women. "You look like you've been on the trail for quite some time," Grace went on. "How about a nice hot bath and a little female companionship?"

White Elk had to admit that the prospect was appealing. He had plenty of money. *Why shouldn't I indulge myself?* he thought.

"All right," he answered with a smile.

Grace nodded toward the four young women. "You can have your pick of companions," she said.

Three of the soiled doves brightened their smiles and tried to look more fetching. The only one who did not smile was the strawberry blonde in the silk chemise. She kept the same half-mocking expression on her face. And yet, White Elk could see the interest in her eyes. There was something intriguing about her—

As he strode across the room toward her, she watched him approach. Her hand lay on the back of a velvet armchair, and she held the casual pose. The only concession she made was to tip her head back slightly to meet his gaze.

"What about you?" White Elk demanded as he stopped in front of her.

"What about me?" she answered in a sultry contralto. White Elk sensed that the voice, like her attitude, was a pose, but he had to admit that she was good at it.

"How would you like to give me a bath?"

"Would you like that?" she replied.

He cupped her chin to hold her head still and brought his mouth down on hers. Her lips responded to his kiss immediately. The only points of contact between them were his fingers on her chin and his mouth pressed hotly to hers, but they were enough. Waves of sensation cascaded through him.

A moment later, he pulled away, careful not to let her see what an effort it was. With a surge of satisfaction, he saw that her firm breasts were rising and falling rapidly.

"You'll do," White Elk said casually.

He slipped an arm around her trim waist and turned to face Grace Pinkston. The madam was still smiling. "Rita, you treat this gentleman nice," she said. "He's a special customer, you know."

"Of course, Grace," the girl said.

"I assume you'll want some payment now," White Elk commented to the madam. Such a question might be a breach of whorehouse etiquette—the business arrangements were usually conducted with the woman who was being hired— but something told White Elk these were unusual circumstances.

Grace shook her head. "We'll talk about that later," she replied. "You just relax and enjoy yourself."

White Elk shrugged and nodded. Nevertheless, he felt a little uncertain about embarking on this debauch without knowing what it would cost him. If Grace named too high a price later on, he could simply pay her what he thought was right and ride on.

Grace turned and called down the hall. "Malachi!"

A short black man with massive shoulders appeared from the back of the house. "Yes, Miz Grace?" he asked. His close-cropped hair was gray, but his smooth dark skin was unlined. The muscles of his arms and shoulders bulged against the work shirt he wore.

White Elk grimaced. If he complained about the price levied by Grace Pinkston, it would probably fall to Malachi to collect it. He decided that taking on the squat, obviously powerful man would be quite a task.

"Heat some bath water for Mr. Duquesne,"

Grace ordered. "Then take a tub up to Rita's room."

Malachi nodded, then glanced in surprise at White Elk. "Duquesne?" he asked.

"That's right," Grace said curtly. Her tone indicated that no more questions were to be asked. Malachi nodded and disappeared down the hall.

White Elk was very aware of Rita's hip pressed against his. Since he had chosen Rita, the other women had lost interest in him, but they still wore professional smiles on their lovely faces. White Elk took one last look at the lush display of creamy flesh, then allowed Rita to lead him to the stairs.

His excitement grew as they went up to the second floor of the house. The subtle fragrance of Rita—the mixture of some perfume and her own natural scent—created an undeniable tension in him.

The carpet runner in the second-floor hall softened and muted their footsteps. The flames in the lanterns attached to the walls were turned low, so they cast a faint glow. Inside the bordello, it might have been the middle of the night—perpetual night, a time for passion and lust—rather than a bright afternoon.

He heard faint sounds coming from behind some of the doors they passed and knew that other prostitutes were practicing their ancient profession in those rooms. He was a bit surprised that he had had the opportunity to choose among four extremely attractive women. Rita was undoubtedly one of the loveliest women he had ever seen, and her haughty air challenged him, yet she had not been chosen by any of the men now locked in passion. That meant that all Grace's women must be stunningly beautiful.

They were halfway down the hall when one of the doors opened suddenly, and a brawny man sporting a distinctive, full brown beard stalked out. He scowled angrily as he shrugged into his coat. Hurrying behind him was a young woman with long blond hair, who was covering her nakedness with a sheet that she had wrapped around her.

"Don't worry about it, Hutch," she said urgently. "I'm sure it was my fault. I-I just didn't do the right things. . . . But you've still got to pay."

The man stopped abruptly when he noticed White Elk and Rita coming toward him. He frowned, and as he realized that White Elk and Rita had heard what the blond woman had said, his expression became angry.

He whirled around to face her. "Shut up, you slut!" he growled. "I paid you what you're worth, which is nothing."

The prostitute clutched at the sleeve of his coat. "But, Hutch—"

He jerked away from her and glanced over his shoulder at White Elk. As Hutch focused on his face, the scout saw the man's eyes narrowing. He stopped as Hutch snapped, "Hey, boy, what's a redskin like you doing here?"

White Elk knew that Hutch's failure with the woman had enraged him, but Hutch was also one of those customers who would be offended by someone with Indian blood. It would be best to ignore him, and White Elk could tell from the way that

Rita squeezed his arm that she did not want trouble either.

"Excuse us, please," White Elk said. He began to move around Hutch.

Hutch reached out and grabbed White Elk's arm. "I asked you what you're doing here!" he snarled.

Unable to suppress his anger, White Elk smiled thinly. "I'm about to do what you evidently can't."

Hutch stared at him as if he could not believe what he had just heard, and his face darkened with fury. "You damned heathen!" he sneered. He clenched his free hand into a fist and swung it toward White Elk's face.

"Malachi!" the blond woman screamed.

White Elk did not wait for help. He jerked his arm out of Hutch's grip, moved smoothly away, and let the wild punch slide harmlessly past his head. Hutch staggered, thrown off-balance by the miss, and White Elk moved in on him. Grasping Hutch's other arm, he stepped behind him and brought the arm up painfully against the man's back. Hutch swore angrily and attempted to twist out of the grip. But the sudden cold touch of a bowie knife against his throat stopped him.

"I don't want trouble, mister," White Elk hissed into the man's ear. "I'm tired and dirty, and I've been promised a bath. I'd like to take it in peace. Why don't you just pay your bill and go about your business?"

A moment went by, then Hutch drew a shaky breath and said, "All right. Just get that knife away from my neck."

White Elk drew the bowie away from his throat

and released his arm. Stepping back quickly, he held the knife up and ready in case Hutch tried anything else. The man merely worked his shoulders, rubbed his stiff arm, and glowered at them.

Malachi appeared at the head of the stairs. He carried no weapon in his hands, but he was plainly ready to deal with any trouble. He paused when he saw the four figures standing in the hall.

"It's all right, Malachi," Rita said. "Just a misunderstanding." She glanced at Hutch for confirmation.

He nodded grudgingly. Reaching into his pocket, he pulled out a coin and slapped it in the blond prostitute's outstretched palm. "That's right," he growled. "Just a misunderstanding." With one last murderous glance at White Elk, he stalked down the hall, pushed past Malachi, and disappeared down the stairs.

White Elk slipped his bowie back into its sheath. He met Malachi's shrewd eyes, and the black man nodded his thanks.

"I really appreciate it, mister," the blond woman said. "That fella's nothing but trouble. I don't know why Grace doesn't just tell him not to come back—"

"You'd best let Miz Grace make those decisions, Lindy," Malachi said sternly. Turning to White Elk, he went on, "I'll have that bath water up here in just a bit, sir."

White Elk nodded. "That's fine."

He glanced down as he felt the blond woman put her hands on his arm. Smiling coyly at him, she said huskily, "Did I hear Malachi say something about a bath? I've been told I'm pretty good at washing things."

Rita laughed sharply and moved between White Elk and the blonde. "Forget it, Lindy. The gentleman's with me."

Lindy shrugged. "I thought it was worth a try."

"Not tonight it isn't," Rita replied, her tone containing a clear warning. As Lindy slipped into her room, Rita linked arms with White Elk and continued leading him down the hall. "Thanks for handling that so smoothly," she said. "Grace doesn't like trouble in the house."

"I told the man the truth," White Elk said. "I don't want trouble; I just want that bath." He glanced up and down the hall. "I notice that nobody else came running to help."

"One of Grace's rules is that the girls stay in their rooms during any kind of trouble. That way they don't get in the path of any stray bullets."

"A good policy," White Elk said dryly.

Rita paused at the last door on the right, opened it, and stepped back to let him precede her. An instinctive caution made White Elk tell her to go ahead. She walked into the room and turned to face him. The lamp on the table beside the bed glowed behind her, and her body was plainly silhouetted through her garment's sheer fabric, making her more appealing than if she had been totally nude.

White Elk gently closed the door behind him and waited. After a moment, Rita came to him. She rested her hands against his chest and lifted her face to be kissed. White Elk pressed his lips to hers and pulled her tightly to him. As he felt himself responding, he slid a hand down her back to her soft hips and pressed her against him. She moaned deeply.

The soft knocking on the door went unheeded for a long moment. Then White Elk broke the kiss and turned his head. "Come in," he said hoarsely.

Malachi opened the door and brought in a large metal tub, which he placed in the center of the floor. "Here you go, sir," he said in his gravelly voice. "I'll be back in a moment with the hot water."

White Elk nodded. As Malachi left the room, White Elk turned back to Rita. His fingertips stroked the smooth skin of her cheek.

"You enjoy this, don't you?" he asked softly. "This is more than just a job to you."

"Sometimes I do," she replied, returning his frank gaze. "I don't know any reason why a girl shouldn't like her work. Do you?"

Slowly, White Elk shook his head.

They stood looking at each other until Malachi returned. He poured steaming buckets of hot water into the tub and then left with a smile and a nod of his grizzled head.

"Why don't you get undressed?" Rita asked huskily.

White Elk smiled at her. "Why don't you do it for me?"

She kept her chemise on as she stripped him. A few times, she paused as she saw the scars that he had collected over the years. "You've been in a few fights," she said as she traced what remained of one long arrow wound on his thigh.

"More than a few," White Elk replied. The touch of her fingers was maddening to him, and he did not know how much he could stand.

When she had removed the dusty, sweat-stiffened buckskins, she dropped them in a corner. "We'll get those clean later," she said, "after you're taken care of."

He stepped into the tub, sinking with a grateful sigh into the hot water. It felt wonderful and immediately soothed the muscle aches that came from the long days in the saddle. He leaned as far back as he could and sank until the water was nearly up to his chest.

Rita had picked up a bar of soap from the small dressing table that sat against one wall and walked slowly toward him.

"You start washing me and that silk outfit's going to get water splashed on it," White Elk warned.

Rita paused and sighed. "You're right," she said. "Here, catch." She tossed the soap to him.

Snatching the soap out of the air, White Elk grinned as, in one graceful, sensuous movement, she peeled the garment down and off and tossed it casually over the foot of the bed.

Nude, she was every bit as lovely as he had expected her to be. She came to the tub, lifted a foot, and slowly slid it into the water.

"Going to be a tight fit in here," White Elk said, looking up at her.

"Yes, indeed," Rita replied huskily.

A muscle jumped in his jaw. "The hell with this,"

he said as he reached for her. He caught her arm and pulled her down. Her foot slipped in the tub, and she sat with a splash, filling his arms with warm, wet, firm flesh.

Neither of them noticed when the water began to cool.

Chapter Four

RITA AND WHITE ELK SPENT THE REST OF THE DAY IN that room. But as fragrant aromas wafted up the stairs, they realized they were hungry for things other than each other. Rita reluctantly left him to go to the kitchen and bring back dinner on a tray. They enjoyed the meal in her big bed.

When he and Rita were finally sated, it was sometime far into the night. White Elk lay peacefully against the pillows. The strawberry blonde was nestled beside him sound asleep with her head resting against his chest. For the first time since he had entered the room, he looked around at the dimly lit scene.

He had been in rooms like this before. The main item of furniture was the bed, and this was one of the most comfortable he had ever encountered. Two thick feather mattresses were stacked on an iron bedstead. Beside the bed was the small table that held the lamp; nearby was a dressing table. In front of it stood a chair with a curved back and a padded seat. An ornate mirror hung above the dressing table, and on the opposite wall was a framed picture, a duplicate of one of the paintings downstairs. Beneath it stood a ladderback chair. The single window was heavily curtained, like the others he had seen in the house.

All in all, it was a much nicer room than some he had seen. And Rita Nevins was no ordinary soiled dove.

She had claimed to enjoy her work, and White Elk was more than convinced of that. Unless she was the best actress in the world, she had thoroughly relished their lovemaking, throwing herself into the passionate coupling with a hot, heady fervor.

Sighing contentedly, he snuggled closer to her and began to doze. Just before he slipped into an exhausted sleep, a thought crossed his mind. If sending him to Grace Pinkston's boardinghouse had been his father's idea of a joke, it had certainly backfired. Pierre could not have sent him to a better place.

The next evening, White Elk put on the buckskins that had been cleaned as Rita had promised and glanced in the mirror one last time. He nodded, satisfied by the relaxed, confident image that looked back at him. He was prepared.

An hour earlier Malachi had brought word that

Grace wanted to see him. The bill has come due, he had thought wryly as he closed the door on the departing man. For over twenty-four hours, he had enjoyed Rita's favors, eaten fine meals, drunk champagne, and slept on clean sheets. The tab would be high.

After Malachi delivered the message, Rita had left quickly to give White Elk a chance to wash, shave, and dress. Now as he walked toward the stairs he could feel a pleasant fatigue in his muscles.

Malachi stood waiting for him at the foot of the stairs. "This way, sir," he said quickly as he gestured toward the rear of the house.

White Elk slipped one of the high quality cigars that Rita had brought to him earlier from his pocket and stuck it in his mouth. He lit it, savoring it, and blew a cloud of smoke toward the ceiling. He wanted to put off this meeting with Grace for a few moments longer.

"I thought I might get a drink first," he said, nodding toward the parlor. He knew from what Rita had said that champagne was always available there.

"Miz Grace wants to see you right away, sir," Malachi replied, as he smoothly insinuated himself between White Elk and the parlor doorway.

The scout drew on the cigar once more and frowned. "Could it be that she doesn't want me in the parlor to upset the other customers with my Indian blood?" he asked.

"I really wouldn't know, Mr. Duquesne." Malachi smiled thinly. "Some folks can be rather intolerant. Or so I've heard."

White Elk chuckled. He really did not want to make things difficult for Malachi. "All right. Let's go talk to Mrs. Pinkston."

Grace Pinkston's small office was at the end of the hallway next to the kitchen. When White Elk entered, she looked up from her desk and smiled warmly at him. "How has your stay been so far, Mr. Duquesne? Everything satisfactory?"

"Very much so," White Elk answered honestly.

"And Rita's been treating you well?"

He nodded. "This has been one of the pleasantest times I've had in years, ma'am. And now, I suppose, we have to discuss payment."

"Indeed," Grace replied. "Malachi, would you step outside for a moment?"

The black man nodded and went out, closing the door behind him. White Elk glanced at the door, then looked levelly at Grace. "Well?" he said. "We might as well get this over with."

"Of course . . . Mr. Duquesne, we cannot accept your money. It is no good here. I don't want to hear another word about your paying for anything. Is that understood?"

White Elk stared at her in disbelief. The madam telling him that he did not have to pay for these luxuries. Impossible!

"You don't want money?" he asked when he finally recovered his composure and his voice.

"That's right," Grace said with a slow nod. "I can't explain further, Mr. Duquesne, but you can stay here free of charge for as long as you like."

She was not joking; she was telling the truth. Perhaps this had something to do with his fracas with the man called Hutch. "I seem to have stumbled into heaven without knowing it." He grinned broadly.

Grace's smile widened. "I suppose that would make Rita an angel. Why don't you find her and tell her so, Mr. Duquesne?"

White Elk clamped the cigar between his teeth and grinned. "I'll do just that," he declared.

Sauntering down the hallway, he stopped at the parlor entrance and scanned the softly lit room for the cloud of strawberry-blond hair. Cigar smoke and laughter filled the air. Several men were enjoying the company of the women before choosing the ones they wished to take upstairs. A couple of the clients grimaced when they noticed the buckskinned half-breed standing in the doorway, but no one said anything.

Wearing the impudent smile that seemed to be her trademark, Rita met him at the doorway and handed him the glass of champagne she was carrying.

"I just told Grace that you were an angel," White Elk said, sipping the champagne.

Rita laughed lightly. "A fallen angel, maybe."

"No," White Elk said, lifting a hand to stroke her cheek. "A real one."

She flushed, unaccustomed to hearing such sincerity from the men she met here. White Elk smiled down at her for a moment, then grinned broadly and slid an arm around her waist. "Come on," he said, gently urging her toward the stairs. The crude hilarity in the parlor did not appeal to him, not when he could be alone with Rita.

Grace had implied he would be free to sample the charms of any of the women, but he had what he wanted, right in the curve of his arm.

The next day White Elk decided to leave the bordello. He knew he should have gone to see his father and Lora before this, but it had been hard to tear himself away from the perfumed delights at Grace's house. A man could not make love, drink champagne, eat fine food, and sleep on silk sheets all the time, he thought as he saddled his horse. Malachi had put the animal in the stable behind the house that first afternoon and had been taking care of it ever since.

Rather than ride directly to his father's house, White Elk decided to spend a little time taking a better look at Abilene. He walked his horse a couple of blocks out of the way to the town's main thoroughfare. As he rode up Texas Street, he saw that the place was bustling. Abilene was a fine, growing city where a man could settle down and raise a family.

Even as he made the observation, he realized he would not be able to stand such an existence. He had spent too much time alone in wide open spaces where there was not another human being within twenty miles. Living a life like that made a man feel stifled when he came to a city.

As White Elk walked his horse down the street, he heard Cody Fisher hail him from the boardwalk in front of the café. White Elk swung his horse toward him and nodded a greeting as he reined in.

"Howdy," Cody said. "Didn't know if you were

still in town, Mr. Duquesne. The marshal and I haven't seen you since you rode in the other day."

"I've been around," White Elk replied. He instinctively liked the young deputy, but he did not want to explain his activities of the last few days.

"Can I buy you a drink?" Cody went on, a friendly grin on his face. "Orion's Tavern down in the next block has the best whiskey in town."

White Elk returned the smile. "Thanks, Deputy, but I'll have to take you up on that some other time. Right now I'm on my way to visit my father and his wife."

"Suit yourself. Anytime you're around, the first one's on me."

With a nod, White Elk urged his horse into a walk. As he rode down the street, he saw the tavern Cody had mentioned next to a small house with a doctor's shingle hanging on a post in front of it. Boisterous laughter floated past the batwing doors of the saloon. At any other time, White Elk would have accepted Cody's offer, but today he felt drawn to his father's house.

He turned north and headed toward Third Street. As the house came into view, he realized how eager he was to visit there again—not so much to see Pierre, but to see Lora.

As he tethered his horse, he noticed her come onto the porch. The bright, wide smile on her face was visible from the street, and he wondered if she had been waiting for him. He hoped that she was not offended because he had not returned sooner.

"White Elk," she scolded as he came onto the porch, "we thought you had gone without saying good-bye to us!" Her warm expression relieved any sting the sharp words might have inflicted.

"I know," he said sheepishly. "I'm sorry, Lora. I've been busier than I expected to be since I got here."

"Busy?" she asked with a puzzled frown. "But I thought you didn't know anyone in Abilene."

"Well . . . something came up that needed my attention. Nothing to worry about." He did not want to lie to her, but at the same time, he was not about to tell her that he had spent the last forty-eight hours in a whorehouse—a whorehouse that her husband had recommended.

Lora took his arm. "Come on inside. I'm sure Pierre will be glad to see you."

The curtains in the parlor had been pulled open, and bright midday sunlight flooded the room. Pierre was sitting on the divan with a newspaper in his hands, and he looked up from the dense columns of fine print as Lora and White Elk came into the room.

"Hello, son." His voice was friendlier than White Elk had expected it to be. "How are you?"

"I'm fine," White Elk said. He waited for his father to say something about thinking that he had left Abilene, but no such comment was forthcoming.

"Have any trouble finding a place to stay?" Pierre asked casually.

"Not at all. I found a good place, and I'm very happy," White Elk answered honestly. He said nothing else, but he watched Pierre for some sort of reaction.

There was none, other than a grunted, "That's good."

Lora still held White Elk's arm. She squeezed it and asked, "You'll stay for lunch, won't you?"

He nodded. He had expected an invitation and had told Rita and Grace that he would not be back until later in the day. He had not explained where he was going.

"I'd be glad to," he said. "I've been remembering that meal you prepared a couple of days ago. There's nothing like home cooking."

That was not true—White Elk had discovered that Malachi could hold his own with anyone in a kitchen—but he was glad to see Lora smile brightly at the compliment.

"You just sit down and have a chat with Pierre," Lora told him. "I'll put another plate on the table."

As Lora bustled from the room, White Elk felt his father's eyes on him. Turning to face him, White Elk said in a low voice, "I suppose I should thank you."

"For what?" Pierre asked, rustling his newspaper as he folded it and put it down on the table in front of him.

"For recommending Grace Pinkston's."

A smile twitched at Pierre's mouth. "Enjoying yourself, are you?"

White Elk sat in one of the armchairs and rested an ankle on his other knee. "You know I've been enjoying it," he said. "I'd wager you're pretty familiar with the place yourself, from the reaction that your name got there."

"Wouldn't know anything about it," Pierre answered curtly. He gestured toward the dining room, where they could hear Lora placing another plate on the table.

White Elk nodded in understanding. He did not want to upset Lora any more than Pierre did.

"You planning to head back to the Army pretty soon?" Pierre asked.

White Elk leaned back in his chair and relaxed. "I'm not sure," he said. "I don't miss the work as much as I thought I would. But I'm not used to sleeping under a roof as much as I have been either." He searched his father's face. "Why do you ask, Pa? Do you want me to stay around?"

Pierre stared at him for a long moment, then said, "I ain't been pining away for you all these years, if that's what you mean, boy. You do what you want. It's none of my damn business."

White Elk was about to agree with him when light footsteps in the hallway announced Lora's return. She stopped in the doorway and said, "Lunch is ready, gentlemen."

"I hope my showing up hasn't put you out," White Elk said as he stood up.

"Nonsense. We have plenty. And we're always glad to see you."

They had a lot of food and everything else, too, White Elk reflected as he sat down at the linen-covered table. This house was furnished with taste and elegance, and that took money. More money than a freight wagon driver should have had.

He wondered what Pierre had been doing before he moved to Abilene. He would not have put it past his father to have been involved in something shady. The money that had paid for this house and its furnishings could have come only from illegal activities.

Asking Pierre about it would do no good, and he knew it. The old man would be stone-faced and silent. White Elk had seen Pierre react that way when he did not want to discuss something.

This meal was as good as the first one. Once again, Pierre did not join in the conversation very often, but White Elk was able to coax a few details about his work from him. It seemed that Pierre took jobs only when he felt like it, which seemed to be only once every couple of weeks. White Elk's curiosity grew, along with his feelings of unease.

Somehow, sitting in this house with Lora—when he had just come from the bed of a perfumed prostitute—embarrassed him. The occasional knowing grin that passed over his father's face did not help matters, especially when Lora asked him again what he had been doing with his time. White Elk fumbled for a moment, then gave her a noncommital answer, while Pierre all but chuckled. White Elk cursed under his breath.

Lora was the personification of innocence and delicacy to him. The last thing he wanted was to have her find out what he had really been doing. In her advanced stage of pregnancy, such upsetting news might be dangerous.

If Lora sensed the growing tension around the table, she said nothing. When they had finished the meal, White Elk offered to help her clear the table. "Thank you," she said, accepting his assistance this time. "I am a little tired today."

As he carried some of the dishes into the kitchen, he asked hesitantly, "How long before . . . ?"

"Oh, soon," Lora answered with a smile. "It can't be too soon for me, though. I can't wait to see this child, to hold it and feed it and love it."

The radiance in her eyes warmed White Elk to the core of his being. The baby would be getting a fine mother. "I'll help you wash these," White Elk said as he stacked the dishes on the counter.

"That's not necessary," Lora assured him. "I'll sit down and rest for a while, and then I'll be fine. I can handle these dishes, White Elk."

He shrugged. "If you're sure . . ."

"Of course I am. Now, you go in and talk to Pierre. I think he'd enjoy that."

Pierre was seated on the divan in the parlor, reading his newspaper. White Elk stood in the doorway and said, "I'd better be going."

Without looking up, Pierre nodded. "Suit yourself."

The snide tone in Pierre's voice raised White Elk's hackles. He glanced down the hall and heard Lora clattering dishes in the kitchen. "Anybody you want me to say hello to for you?" he asked in a low voice.

Pierre's jaw tightened, and he looked angrily at his son. "You always were quick to speak your mind, boy. I never liked that in you."

With a grin, White Elk reached for his hat. "Say good-bye to Lora for me." He went out, shutting the door quietly behind him.

It would be good to get back to Grace's. If he spent too much time around Lora, he might get used to behaving like a normal man with a family, instead of the loner who had learned how to protect himself from all of the world's hurts.

As White Elk made love to Rita that afternoon, his life as an Army scout seemed very far away. The passion he felt while he was in her embrace erased his ugly memories of the hardships and dangers. It also made him forget the problems he had had in the past with his father.

He was still not sure why Pierre had sent him to Grace's, but he was thankful that he had not heeded the warning of that store clerk on Texas Street.

With Rita nestled in his arms, White Elk lay back against the soft pillows, content to close his eyes and relax. Idly, he stroked the smooth skin of her hip, then slid his hand up to her hair. As the silky strands slipped through his fingers, he realized that he was wondering how it would feel to hold Lora in his arms instead of Rita.

Rita felt him stiffen and lifted her head from his shoulder. "What is it?" she whispered. "Is something wrong?"

White Elk's eyes snapped open, and with a shake of his head he banished the unbidden image. His breathing felt harsh in his throat. "It's nothing," he said hoarsely. "Nothing's wrong."

"For a second I thought you were going to jump out of your skin," Rita murmured. She settled against him and began caressing his chest. "You wouldn't want to do that."

White Elk did not reply. He lay silently while Rita went to sleep. Within moments he heard her deep, regular breathing. She was tired, and with good reason. They had been busy since he had arrived.

Despite his own fatigue, he could not sleep. He was a man who could easily nap in territory overrun by hostile Comanches, but now, suddenly, he was afraid to give in to slumber. He stared at the wallpaper pattern and saw that the paper was beginning to fade. During the next few hours he became very familiar with it.

He somehow knew that if he slept, he would dream. And in those dreams would be the alluring, forbidden face of Lora Duquesne.

"I hope you'll pardon me for saying so, sir, but you look like hell."

White Elk grinned tiredly at Malachi as he paused at the bottom of the stairs. "I feel like it, too," he said. "I thought I might sleep a little this afternoon, but it didn't work out that way."

Malachi nodded in understanding, or what he thought was understanding, and White Elk did not bother to correct the impression the black man obviously had. What other conclusion was anybody supposed to draw? They *were* in a whorehouse, after all.

From the sound of the raucous laughter that came from the parlor, a good crowd was on hand this evening. White Elk had heard that some of the women were jealous of Rita and the time she spent with him. He was flattered, but he would not let it go to his head. He had wondered what would happen if someone wanted to hire Rita, but so far he had not faced that problem. While he had received plenty of special treatment, he was not sure where Grace would draw the line.

More importantly, he could not predict what his reaction would be. He would not fool himself into thinking that he had fallen in love with Rita, but he was genuinely fond of her.

This evening he had traded his buckskins for a pair of dark pants and a plain white shirt. He knew the clothes made his Kiowa heritage a little less obvious, but that was not the reason he had worn them. He simply felt the need for a change. Tonight, he wanted to be just another customer— albeit a non-paying one—rather than the half-breed scout who had tracked Quanah Parker to Palo Duro Canyon.

"Could I get you a drink, sir?" Malachi asked as White Elk strolled toward the parlor.

"I'll manage," White Elk replied. Getting a drink was no problem; several bottles of champagne were always being passed around the parlor, and a willing serving girl was usually close at hand.

Malachi nodded and drifted back toward the kitchen. As White Elk watched him go, he realized that he had not eaten in a while. One of the black man's sumptuous meals would taste good, but first he would have that drink.

As he stepped into the parlor, White Elk's gaze darted around the room. Out of habit, he noted where the men were positioned and looked for signs of trouble. Almost a dozen men were scattered around the room, along with an equal number of young women. Although the women were scantily dressed as usual, there was nothing happening other than talking and laughing and an occasional stolen kiss. The more serious activities were reserved for the upstairs rooms. Grace Pinkston sat in an armchair near the parlor's entrance, hands folded demurely in her lap, watching her patrons when she was not answering the frequent knocks on the front door.

White Elk absorbed all of that in a split second, and then he stiffened as he looked again through the smoky haze and saw the man on the other side of the room. He was sitting on a sofa, talking to one of the prostitutes while he caressed her bare shoulder. He seemed to sense eyes on him, and he looked up abruptly. His full brown beard quivered as his jaw tightened.

Hutch's fingers clutched the woman's shoulder, and she bit her lip to keep from crying out. As he stood up, he removed his hand, revealing the ugly red imprints of his fingers on her soft skin.

White Elk froze and met Hutch's angry gaze.

Hutch squared his shoulders and reached out to tap one of the other men on the shoulder. "Look," he said when his companion had turned away from the raven-haired woman he had been talking to. Hutch went on in a voice loud enough to be heard by everyone in the room, "It's that damned redskin I told you about."

Suddenly the talking and laughter died. Several other men, obviously friends of Hutch, muttered angrily as they looked at White Elk standing in the doorway.

Grace was on her feet. "Mr. Murphy!" she said sharply. "I told you that you could return to this establishment only if you promised not to cause any more trouble. I'll thank you to keep your promise."

"A promise to a whore don't mean nothing," Hutch snorted.

The madam went pale under her rouge. White Elk glanced around the room and noticed that most of the customers were edging away from Hutch. But four men moved to his side.

A grim smile tugged at White Elk's mouth. Five to one—bad odds, but not the worst he had ever faced. Hutch and his friends might beat him, but they would not be unscathed.

"Mind if I lend a hand, sir?" asked a gravelly voice behind him. White Elk took his eyes off Hutch long enough to glance back and see Malachi standing there. The black man's face was solemn, but his dark eyes twinkled in anticipation. Obviously he was looking forward to a scrap.

Before White Elk could reply, Grace said, "I don't want a lot of damage in here, Malachi."

"Of course, Miz Grace."

White Elk looked back at Hutch. "If you want trouble, I'll be glad to oblige, mister. But let's move outside first."

Hutch nodded curtly. "Sure. Why not?"

White Elk started to turn away. They could go out back, between the house and the stable—

"White Elk! Look out!" cried one of the prostitutes.

The scout spun around and instinctively lifted his hands as Hutch lunged across the room at him. The bearded man threw a wild punch at White Elk's head, but the scout blocked it easily. Hutch's rush made White Elk step back involuntarily, and he tried to set himself to return the blow.

Hutch's four companions hurtled forward. One of them banged roughly into White Elk's side and knocked him further off-balance. At the same moment, Malachi entered the fracas. He grabbed one man by the arm, spun him around, and smashed a fist into his face.

White Elk hooked his balled fist into Hutch's belly, and the man's liquor-laden breath puffed into his face. He followed it with a short, powerful punch that rocked Hutch's head back. But at the same time Hutch's companions were hammering him with their fists. One of them clipped White Elk on the jaw, staggering him and forcing him onto one knee. A booted foot crashed into his ribs. As the force of the blow stunned him, he sprawled full length on the carpeted floor.

White Elk was vaguely aware of women shouting and screaming, and he heard Malachi roar as the burly black man fought. With a burst of effort, the scout got his hands under him and pushed himself over, just in time to roll out of the path of another kick, this one from a livid Hutch. He grasped Hutch's ankle as it went by, and twisted it hard so that the man yelped and fell heavily.

Another roll brought White Elk lithely to his feet. As he saw Malachi fighting with two of Hutch's friends, he noticed a third man moving behind the knot of struggling figures. This man slipped a pistol from his pocket and flipped it around so that he was clutching the barrel and the cylinder. As he lifted it over his head, White Elk shouted, "Behind you, Malachi!"

The black man jerked his head around and tried to move away when he saw the new threat, but he was too late. The butt of the pistol thudded into the side of his head. Malachi staggered, and his legs folded under him.

Blazing with fury, White Elk lunged toward the man who had struck Malachi. A brawl with fists was one thing; he was used to that. But trying to cave in a man's head with a gun butt was something entirely different.

He did not reach the man with the gun. As he went by Hutch, a foot suddenly thrust between his legs made him fall again. In a flash, Hutch was pounding his fists into White Elk's face. Now that Malachi was out of the fight, all the men could concentrate on White Elk. The scout knew he was finished, but at least he had put up a good fight.

A sudden fear gripped him. If he were beaten to death in this bordello, Lora would certainly hear of it sooner or later. The realization gave him new strength.

White Elk surged up. He threw Hutch to the side, buried a fist in another man's stomach, and whirled to smash a third man in the face.

"Shoot the son of a bitch!" Hutch howled.

The man with the pistol was just as caught up in the battle as Hutch, and he had fallen back when White Elk exploded up off the floor. Now he stood by the parlor entrance, a good eight feet away. He lifted the pistol and aimed it at White Elk. Cold fear clutched at White Elk's belly as he realized he could not tackle the man in the time it would take him to pull the trigger.

A hand came down on the gunman's shoulder

before he could fire. The man was jerked around, and a hard fist crashed into his jaw. He fell to the floor; the pistol slipped out of his hand and clattered away, unfired. A tall figure appeared in the doorway, face dark with anger.

White Elk gaped as he watched his father throw himself into the fight. In one fluid motion, Pierre knocked aside one of Hutch's friends and grabbed another in a bear hug.

The scout had no more time to wonder what Pierre Duquesne was doing here. The furious Hutch and the remaining man renewed their charge. White Elk blocked the man's punch, grabbed his shirtfront, and jerked him close enough to smash a knee into the man's groin. That left Hutch, who suddenly looked a little green, standing alone.

White Elk launched a flurry of blows that forced Hutch to back up and block them desperately. The scout was only setting him up. A second later, when White Elk feinted to his left, Hutch tried to dodge away and moved right into an uppercut that had White Elk's full force behind it.

The fist caught Hutch on the jaw and lifted him off the floor. His feet went up in the air as he flew backward and crashed onto the carpet. He sprawled, utterly still.

White Elk drew a deep breath and turned to see that his father had enjoyed equal success. Both of Pierre's opponents were stretched out on the floor. Only one of the five men who had jumped White Elk was still conscious, and he lay curled in a tight ball, moaning and clutching where White Elk's knee had savaged him.

A grin suddenly stretched across White Elk's face as he looked at Pierre. "Thanks," he said. "That was a pretty good fight, but it could've gotten unpleasant if you hadn't shown up when you did."

Pierre snorted contemptuously as he looked around. "The Army must've made you soft, boy, if you can't kick five dogs like this by yourself."

White Elk could not tell if Pierre was serious. He ignored the gibe and bent to slip an arm around Malachi's shoulders. The black man was groaning and shaking his head. White Elk helped him into a sitting position.

"Are you all right, Malachi?" the scout asked. "Maybe I should fetch a doctor."

Malachi shakily lifted a hand and probed at the lump on his head. "Thanks anyway, sir, but this old noggin's taken worse licks than that. I'll be all right."

White Elk helped him to his feet and then turned to face the angry gaze of Grace Pinkston. "I tried to talk them into taking their fight outside, Mrs. Pinkston," he said. "You heard me, and you saw how they jumped us."

Grace nodded. She peered around the room, where the prostitutes and the remaining customers were huddling in careful silence. Finally, Grace said, "I don't see any harm done. We were lucky this time. I can promise you one thing—Hutch Murphy will not bring his trade to this house any more."

"Damn right he won't," Pierre growled. "Malachi, give me a hand tossing this trash into the street." He bent to grasp the feet of one of the unconscious men and hauled him out of the parlor.

White Elk stared after him. There had been a definite tone of command in his father's voice. Why was Pierre Duquesne giving orders in Grace's house? For that matter, what was he doing here in the first place? White Elk could not deny that Pierre's arrival had probably saved his life, but he wanted some answers.

Grace put a hand on his arm. "Come on," she said, her tone much gentler. "You've got a pretty good scrape on your face. Let's go to the kitchen and put something on it."

He let her lead him to the kitchen and sat in the straight-backed chair she indicated. Moving to a cabinet, she took a bottle of whiskey and splashed some of the liquor on a cloth. The whiskey fumes were strong in White Elk's nose as she swabbed his face.

"I imagine that burns a little," she said.

"Some," he grunted. Without looking up at her, he went on, "What's my father doing here, Grace?"

The madam hesitated before she answered. Finally, she said, "Maybe he came for the same reason any other man does."

Something had occurred to White Elk, and he glanced at the back door to confirm it. "I didn't hear him come in the front. He just appeared out of nowhere."

"You were fighting; I'm not surprised you didn't hear him come in." Grace stepped back, lowering the whiskey-soaked cloth.

White Elk nodded toward the back door, which was still slightly ajar. "Or else Pierre was slipping in the back when he heard that brawl in the parlor and ran to lend a hand. What's going on here,

Grace? Why was my father slipping in the back door of a house like this?"

Before Grace could answer, the kitchen door opened, and Pierre stepped into the room. He said, "Malachi and I threw all those troublemakers out, Grace, and I warned Murphy not to come back. He's just a bully. You won't have to worry about him anymore."

Grace nodded. "Good," she said fervently. Suddenly, her eyes widened. "My lord, Pierre, you're hurt!"

The Frenchman lifted his right hand and regarded his blood-covered knuckles. "It's nothing," he said. "I just scraped some skin off."

White Elk stared at him. "I want to talk to you, Pa," he said after a moment.

"So talk," Pierre grunted.

"In private."

Pierre considered the request, then shrugged. He gave Grace a meaningful look, and the madam said, "I'd better make sure that everyone has calmed down. We can't have customers frightened off by a little fight." She went into the hall and disappeared toward the parlor.

Pierre looked levelly at White Elk. "What do you want to say to me, boy?"

"I want the answer to one question," White Elk said.

Pierre waited in silence.

"You're not just a regular customer here, are you?"

"No," Pierre said brusquely. "I own the place."

White Elk had half expected that answer, but it

still came as a shock. His father owned one of Abilene's most lucrative whorehouses. As he sat there and thought about it, everything fell into place. Now he knew why he had been given special treatment in the bordello. It also explained where Pierre's money came from. His father's earnings from his infrequent jobs as a freight wagon driver could not have been enough to buy and furnish his house.

Did Lora know? he suddenly wondered. Surely not. She believed Pierre had told her the truth about his life, but now White Elk knew better.

"Say something, dammit!" Pierre suddenly rasped. "Don't just sit there and stare at me."

"I'm not sure what to say," White Elk mused. "Except that this tells me you haven't changed much after all. You're still the same old bastard you always were."

Pierre clenched his fists. "I just saved your life out there, boy," he growled.

"And I said thanks." White Elk stood up.

Pierre caught his arm. "Don't you even think about going to Lora and telling her about this," he said in a low, dangerous voice. "She'd never understand. I'll kill you myself if you don't keep your mouth shut."

White Elk took a deep breath and jerked his arm free. "Don't worry," he said coldly. "I didn't tell Lora when I thought you were just a regular customer. I'm certainly not going to tell her that you own the place. For one thing, I'd have to admit to her that I've been living here."

A humorless grin stretched across Pierre's face.

"You're a hypocrite, boy. You've been eating my food and drinking my liquor and bedding Rita, and now you go and act like there's something wrong with me owning this house. Well, I don't give a damn what you think about me. Never have."

White Elk's chest was tight with anger. Pierre was right. He had thoroughly enjoyed himself when he thought that Grace owned the house. The fact that Pierre was the owner did not change any of the things he had done over the last few days.

"I know you never cared what I thought," he said. "And I don't care what you think, either. Let's keep it that way."

"All right by me," Pierre agreed with a nod.

The kitchen door opened then, and Grace came back into the room. She glanced from father to son, then said, "White Elk, Rita's back from town. I had sent her to the store to pick up some fabric for me, and when she got back the first thing she heard was how you had gotten into a fight with a dozen men." The madam smiled wryly. "The way those townies are talking, it'll be two dozen by tomorrow morning. Anyway, the girl's worried about you. You'd better get out there and let her know that you're all right."

White Elk nodded. "Thanks, Grace. I was wondering where she had gone." He started toward the kitchen door.

Pierre stepped forward and slid an arm around Grace's waist. "Come along, Gracie," he said heartily. "Malachi can keep an eye on things down here. Let's you and me head upstairs."

"Of course, Pierre," she murmured.

White Elk paused in the doorway and briefly met

his father's arrogant gaze. He knew the old man was just trying to irritate him. And Pierre was succeeding, *blast it*.

He shook his head. As he went to look for Rita, he wondered if coming to Abilene had been a serious mistake.

Chapter Five

————◆————

WHEN HE AWOKE THE NEXT MORNING, WHITE ELK was still asking himself that question. As he lay in bed with Rita snuggled warmly against him, he wondered if he should pack his gear, get on his horse, and ride out of Abilene. He could go back to Indian Territory and his old job as a scout. That would be simpler than staying and sorting through the tangled emotions his visit had aroused.

It had been far into the night before he had been able to fall asleep. He lay next to the sleeping Rita and kept reliving the evening's events. He was not sure he could look Lora in the eye again, knowing that Pierre owned this bordello and that she was blissfully unaware of it. But the last thing he wanted to do was hurt Lora. The very last thing . . .

Rita shifted her head against his shoulder and

looked up to find him staring at the wall. She sighed sleepily. "I swear, you're about the moodiest man I ever saw," she said. "Every time I turn around, you're brooding about something."

White Elk put a smile on his face. "Sorry," he told her. "I was just thinking about Pierre."

Rita raised herself on an elbow. The sheet slipped down, exposing her firm breasts. "I told you last night, Grace gave us strict orders not to tell anybody that he owns the house. That included you. I didn't like keeping it from you, but there was nothing I could do."

He placed a fingertip on her lips. "Hush. I know you couldn't tell me. I'm not upset with you."

"You're just angry with him." Rita grasped his finger and kissed it lightly.

"I'm not sure . . ." White Elk could not tell Rita that he was concerned about Lora, not Pierre.

She slid her hand down his body. He knew she was trying to distract him, and right now he was more than willing to let her. He forced his worries from his mind and turned toward her, reveling in her warm, smooth flesh. He let her passion carry him away.

He would not leave Abilene, he decided. Not just yet.

"I tell you, that's him," a young voice hissed.

"No, it ain't. That fella ain't old enough. The way I heard tell, Duquesne's been fighting Injuns for twenty years or more."

"Aw, you're crazy! I know it's him. Agnes told me, and Cody told her."

With his lips twitching, White Elk leaned back in

his chair on the porch of the Grand Palace Hotel. The two young boys were huddled twenty feet away at the edge of the porch, whispering urgently to each other while they stole glances at him. He forced his face to remain expressionless as he listened to their argument. Dressed in his buckskins, he supposed he made a picturesque sight on the main street of town.

When he remembered that it was Saturday afternoon and that the town would be full of people, he felt a restless urge and decided he needed to spend some time outside the bordello. After promising Rita he would return for dinner, he had ridden to Texas Street and found a spot to sit and watch the world go by.

Abilene was busy today. The street was crowded with horses and wagons, and people hurried back and forth on the boardwalk in front of him. Most of the pedestrians were farmers with their families, although a few cowboys appeared in the throng.

Abilene was much like the rest of the West, White Elk thought. Less than a decade earlier, the town had been new and brawling, filled with Texas cowhands, the air punctuated with the roar of gunshots. Then Bear River Tom Smith, Wild Bill Hickok, and now Luke Travis had arrived, and with them came law and order. Once the town had been civilized, storekeepers, farmers, and bankers followed. Most of the time the streets of Abilene were probably as safe—or safer—than those of Eastern cities like Chicago and Philadelphia and New York.

The frontier had moved farther west now. With every year that passed, White Elk mused, more and more territory was settled. The Indians had strongly resisted the white man's advance, and despite Custer's misadventure, within a few years—twenty at most—all the battles would have been fought.

White Elk frowned. Those young boys were so impressed with him because they knew, as well as he did, that Army Indian scouts would soon be gone with the Indians they tracked.

He heard a tentative step on the boardwalk and glanced over to see that the two boys had come closer. The one in the lead was a freckle-faced redhead with a pugnacious jaw and eyes full of mischief. White Elk grinned as the boy said, "Mister, you mind if we ask you a question?"

"Sure, fellas, go right ahead," he replied.

"Are you that scout they call Duquesne?"

White Elk nodded solemnly. "I am."

The boy looked triumphantly at his companion. "Told you, Danny!" he exclaimed. Turning back to White Elk, he went on excitedly, "This here's Danny Sims, and I'm Michael Hirsch."

"Glad to meet you, boys," White Elk replied.

Emboldened by Michael's success at talking to the scout, Danny spoke up. "They say you been fighting Injuns for a long time."

"Oh, not that long. Just a few years, really. Sometimes it just seems like a long time."

"You were in the Red River War, weren't you?" Michael asked.

White Elk nodded. "How did you hear about the Red River War?"

"Shoot, it was in all the papers," Michael replied proudly. "That was before we came to Abilene. All the papers back East wrote about the Injun wars."

Danny peered at White Elk for a long moment,

then said, "You look like you're part Injun yourself, Mr. Duquesne."

"Darn it, Danny, hush up!" Michael whispered and poked his companion in the ribs.

White Elk shook his head. "That's all right, Michael. It just so happens Danny's right. My mother was a Kiowa Indian."

"So you fight against your own folks?" Danny asked brashly. Other children began to appear on the boardwalk, edging closer to hear the conversation between their friends and the buckskin-clad scout.

"I'm half white, too," White Elk explained. "But I have to admit that I did worry about that, Danny. In a lot of ways, the Indians make more sense about things than the white men. But I went to school and studied history, and I could tell that sooner or later the white men were going to come out on top." He shrugged. "And the sooner the fighting is over, the sooner folks will stop dying, white and Indian alike. You understand?"

"I think I do," a new voice said. "You're a pragmatist, Mr. Duquesne."

He turned and saw a stern-faced woman in the black habit of a Dominican nun standing nearby. He stood up quickly, then after a moment nodded and said, "I guess you could say that. You look like you don't approve, Sister."

"I don't approve of these children pestering you, especially when they're neglecting their chores." She waved at the youngsters. "Michael, Danny, you and the others move along now. I'll expect you back at the orphanage shortly."

Grudgingly, the youngsters started to walk away. Michael Hirsch glanced back and said, "So long, Mr. Duquesne. Maybe we can talk some more later."

"I hope so," White Elk said.

When the children had gone, the nun said, "My name is Sister Laurel, Mr. Duquesne. I run the orphanage where most of those children live. I hope they didn't bother you too much."

White Elk shook his head. "No, I like kids, Sister. They're orphans, eh?"

"Most of them. We've established a place for them to live, a healthy environment for them to grow up in."

A grin tugged at White Elk's mouth. "And I suspect you don't think someone like me ought to be part of that healthy environment."

Sister Laurel's expression softened. "I didn't mean to sound so disapproving of you, Mr. Duquesne," she said. "You at least sound like an educated man. The good Lord knows, with all the cowhands and tinhorn gamblers and saloon women in Abilene, an Army scout is . . . is . . ." She seemed to be at a loss for words.

White Elk's grin widened. "No worse than anybody else?" he finished for her. He lifted his hand as she started to protest. "No, Sister, I understand exactly what you're saying. I'm a living reminder of a great deal of violence, my skin color as well as my profession. I am curious, though. You sounded almost as if you were on the side of the Indians a moment ago."

She met his frank gaze. "I'm opposed to violence

except when it's absolutely necessary, Mr. Duquesne. It just seems to me that what you do helps to foster the killing on the frontier."

White Elk's eyes turned bleak with memory. "Then you haven't been out here long enough, Sister. I've watched the soldiers and the Indians killing each other for a long time, and nobody wants a war to end any sooner than the people who are fighting it. I can promise you that."

"I'm glad to hear you say that," Sister Laurel said with a smile. "I've enjoyed talking to you, Mr. Duquesne, but I have to be going now. Otherwise I'll never round up all of those rascals."

White Elk touched the brim of his hat. "Ma'am," he said with a nod.

Leaning against the boardwalk railing, he thoughtfully watched the black-clad nun move down the street. His conversations with the youngsters and with Sister Laurel had certainly not helped him resolve any of the doubts that had been nagging at him. Despite what he had told them, he was not at all sure what he would do with the rest of his life.

As his gaze came to rest on Orion's Tavern two doors away, an answer suggested itself, at least as far as the immediate future was concerned. He would have a drink. He remembered Cody Fisher saying that Orion's served the best whiskey in Abilene.

Next to the Grand Palace was a house set back from the boardwalk behind a neat lawn. This was Dr. Aileen Bloom's office. White Elk glanced at it as he went by and saw several people on their way into the building. Saturday would be a busy day for doctors, too.

Orion's Tavern was a narrow frame structure with the standard batwing doors at its entrance. White Elk pushed them open and paused for a second to let his eyes adjust to the relative dimness inside.

Like most saloons, Orion's was laid out in a simple manner. A long bar with a polished hardwood top ran along the right side; on the wall behind it were shelves filled with bottles of liquor. Scattered throughout the room were tables, some covered with red-checked cloths, the rest bare so that cards could be shuffled and dealt more easily.

A half-dozen laughing, talking cowboys were resting their boots on the brass railing that ran along the bottom of the bar as they tossed back shots of whiskey or sipped from mugs of beer. They shared the tavern with at least that many farmers and a handful of townsmen. At three of the tables, poker games were in progress. White Elk was not surprised that he did not see any women. In a place like this men drank, played cards, and swapped lies. When it was time for female companionship, there were plenty of other places in Abilene to find it—like Grace Pinkston's.

A white-aproned young man with a receding chin was busily pouring drinks behind the bar. At the far end of the bar, a broad-shouldered man with a shaggy, reddish-gray beard was standing next to a wooden perch. A large green parrot clung to the perch, rapidly blinking its eyes as it peered around the room. The bearded man fed it a bit of bread and spoke to it in a rumbling voice. The parrot squawked and then launched into a screeching rendition of a Scots ballad.

White Elk, immediately comfortable, grinned and stepped into the tavern. As he strolled to the bar, he could feel the men in the room study him with frank curiosity; but he did not sense any of the hostility he had encountered in other saloons.

The parrot broke off his song and shrilled, "Devil be damned! Devil be damned!"

The red-bearded man chuckled and said, "Aye." He came around the end of the bar and ambled toward the newcomer. White Elk watched him approach and noticed the obvious strength and power in his burly frame. The man might be middle-aged, but he was far from past his prime.

"Good day to ye, sir," the man said as he stuck out a massive hand. "I be Orion McCarthy, the proprietor o' this here establishment."

"White Elk Duquesne," the scout replied, shaking Orion's hand. "I'm glad to meet you, Mr. McCarthy."

"Call me Orion," the saloonkeeper said. "I been expecting ye. Cody told me he had informed ye o' the excellent libations to be had here."

White Elk grinned. "He did indeed. Said you had the best whiskey in Abilene, in fact."

"And a fact it is!" Orion boomed. He turned to the bartender and called, "Augie! Bring us a bottle an' a couple o' glasses, lad."

While the bartender hurried to bring the whiskey and glasses, White Elk said in a low voice, "Did Fisher also tell you that I have Indian blood, Orion? Legally, I'm not sure you should be serving me."

Orion looked at him and cocked one bushy eyebrow. "I'm a firm believer in law an' order, or at least in the spirit of it. But ye look to me like the kind o' lad who can hold his liquor. I'll ask ye flat out—kin ye handle it?"

White Elk grinned. "I seem to have inherited my capacity from my father rather than my mother, and my father is Pierre Duquesne. I'm told he's sometimes called Frenchy around here. Does that answer your question?"

"Aye, that it does!" Orion clapped a hand exuberantly on White Elk's back, and the younger man staggered slightly. Taking the bottle from Augie, Orion splashed whiskey into the glasses and raised one. "Here's to ye, lad!"

White Elk picked up his drink and tossed it back, savoring the hot bite of the liquor. "Cody was right," he said a moment later. "That is fine whiskey."

Out of the corner of his eye, he noticed a shadow loom in the doorway. Keeping track of such things was a habit that had helped keep him alive and one that he did not want to break. He turned to see who was coming in.

Cody Fisher strode into the tavern. Several patrons called his name and raised beer mugs in greeting. The deputy waved casually and headed for the bar. He grinned broadly at White Elk and said, "I see you decided to try the whiskey."

"You were right," White Elk replied as Orion motioned to Augie to refill their glasses. "It is good."

Cody fished in his pocket and brought out a coin, which he flipped to Augie. "I told you the first round was going to be on me," he said, "and I meant it."

"Here, lad," Orion protested. "I meant for Mr. Duquesne's drink to be on the house."

"You can get the next one," Cody pointed out. "After all, it is your place."

Orion shrugged and nodded. "And the third round is on me," White Elk said.

"I'm not going to argue with that. But I'm one behind. Bring me a glass, Augie," Cody requested.

Orion nodded toward one of the tables. "What say we make ourselves a bit more comfortable, laddies?"

White Elk and Cody followed him to a table. During the next hour Orion refilled their glasses several times, and White Elk found that he was enjoying himself immensely. Cody and Orion were both friendly and full of questions about his experiences as an Army scout.

"Orion and I were in Indian Territory a little while ago," Cody said after White Elk had mentioned being headquartered at the Kiowa reservation there. "Had to chase some train robbers."

"Aye, 'twas a good fight while it lasted," Orion added.

White Elk leaned back in his chair. "I think I heard about that. They kidnapped a girl, too, didn't they?"

"That's right. Had the town in quite an uproar." Cody sipped his whiskey. "Things have settled down now. Abilene's pretty quiet most of the time. Speaking of that, I don't recall you saying what you've been doing with yourself the last few days. I thought you'd have headed back to the Army by now."

White Elk could tell that Cody was asking not as a lawman but as a newfound friend. "I'm not sure I'm going back," he said. "A man gets tired of all the fighting."

Cody and Orion nodded. Both of them had seen their share of violence. As a lawman, Cody dealt with it often. Sudden death was a way of life on the frontier.

"What will ye do if ye don't go back?" Orion asked. "Not that 'tis any o' me business."

White Elk smiled. "I really don't know. That's one of the things I've been thinking about today."

The batwings were pushed open, and three men stepped into the tavern. White Elk glanced at them and found himself looking into the glaring face of Hutch Murphy.

"Goddamn it," Murphy said slowly, loudly, and distinctly in a voice that carried to every man in the room. "I didn't know Orion would let a damn Injun drink in his place. We'll have to stop comin' in here, boys."

"At least 'til the stink's worn off," one of the other men replied with a nasty grin.

White Elk's fingers tightened on his glass, and his jaw set in a taut line. He was in no mood for another battle with the loudmouthed Murphy and his friends.

Cody's eyes darted from White Elk to the newcomers and back. "Take it easy, White Elk," he said in a low voice. "I know those boys, and they'd like nothing better than to prod you into a fight."

"I know that," White Elk replied. "I've already had a run-in with them."

Orion shoved his chair back, the legs rasping on the floor. Moving with surprising agility, he slipped around the table and started toward Hutch and the other men. "Hold on, lads," he said. "I'll have no fighting in me place, not unless I be doing some of it meself."

"Don't worry, McCarthy," Hutch sneered. "I'm tired of dirtying my hands on that filthy half-breed. I just want one quick drink, and then we'll be out of here. All right?"

Orion considered, then shrugged. "Be quick about it," he warned as he jerked his head toward the bar.

Hutch and his friends moved unsteadily to the bar. Obviously they had been sampling whiskey in some other saloon. They ordered drinks from Augie and leaned on the bar without looking at the table where White Elk and Cody sat.

Orion returned to the table, muttering curses under his breath as he sat down. "One of the few disadvantages of owning a tavern," he said to White Elk, "is the people ye sometimes have t'serve."

"I understand," White Elk replied. "I don't want to cause any trouble, Orion. I'll leave if you like."

Orion shook his head. Cody said, "It looked to me like Murphy was the one who wanted to cause trouble. The man's carrying a grudge, White Elk. What happened?"

The scout nodded. "He's carrying a grudge, all right. He and those two and a couple of other men jumped me when I was in— Well, it doesn't matter where I was."

"Five agin one," Orion growled. "Such men are no better'n a pack o' wild dogs."

"A couple of friends of mine helped me out," White Elk said. "We managed to send them packing. To begin with, Murphy doesn't like me because of the color of my skin, and that brawl just made things worse."

Cody nodded. "I'd keep my eyes open, if I were you. I wouldn't put much past Murphy."

"Neither would I," White Elk agreed.

He and the others resumed their drinking, but White Elk continued to watch Murphy cautiously. The men were taking their time with their drinks, but after several minutes they finished the whiskey and turned away from the bar.

Instead of heading toward the door, the trio ambled across the room to the table where White Elk, Cody, and Orion sat. White Elk tensed. Despite the grin on Hutch Murphy's face, the scout was certain that he was coming to make trouble.

Hutch paused beside the table and nodded to Cody. "Howdy, Deputy," he said.

Cody returned the greeting and said, "What can I do for you, Murphy?"

"We just wanted to tell Duquesne here that there're no hard feelings about the other night." Murphy smiled at White Elk as he spoke, but his eyes were as cold and hateful as they had been at Grace's.

White Elk did not believe a word he said. Murphy had been humiliated by his defeat, and the fact that White Elk knew of his failure with the prostitute called Lindy made matters worse. But if Hutch wanted to avoid trouble, that was fine with the scout.

"No hard feelings," White Elk said. He did not extend his hand.

"Glad to hear it," Murphy replied. "Guess we'll be moving along now."

As he started to turn away, Murphy flung his arm out. His hand hit the half-full whiskey bottle sitting on the table and tipped it over so that the liquor spilled directly into White Elk's lap. Murphy glanced back and laughed harshly.

"Looks like I had a little accident," he jeered. "Sorry about that, redskin."

White Elk sat frozen, staring straight ahead as the last of the whiskey gurgled out of the bottle and splashed onto his buckskins. The whole room seemed to hold its breath.

Then White Elk exploded out of his chair. Everything that had happened since he had arrived in Abilene—the two run-ins with Murphy, the friction with his father, his uncertainty about his future—blew up inside White Elk. With a howl of rage, he smashed his fist into Hutch Murphy's face. Murphy staggered back from the blow, and White Elk followed him, swinging more punches.

One of Murphy's friends yelled, "Redskinned bastard!" The man yanked the pistol from his holster and raised it to slash at White Elk's head with the barrel.

In a flash Cody was out of his chair. His strong fingers wrapped around the man's wrist, stopping the blow before it could fall. He wrenched the man around and drove a fist into his belly.

The third man grabbed a chair and started to swing it. Orion lunged at him with a roar, knocked the chair aside, and grappled with him.

Murphy had recovered his balance and was blocking White Elk's punches while throwing some of his own. His fist slammed into White Elk's jaw, knocking the scout backward into a table and upsetting it. Shouting with rage, Murphy followed him, swinging wild punches that missed.

White Elk had not wanted this fight, but it had been forced on him. He felt a pang of regret as he realized the damage they would do to Orion's place. But there was no time for thinking; he had to stop Murphy before the man beat him to death.

Orion's arms went around his opponent's waist; then he picked him up and slung him across the room. The man smashed into Murphy and sent him flying.

At that same moment, Cody was rocked backward by a hard blow to the chin, and he careened into the path of the charging Orion. As they crashed, both men reeled, their feet tangling. Cody fell. Orion maintained his balance, but the effort cost him a punch in the face.

Hutch Murphy charged at White Elk just as Cody pushed himself to his feet. Murphy and Cody collided. They sprawled on the floor and began clawing at each other. In the heat of the battle, Murphy was heedless of the fact that his foe was a lawman. His clutching fingers reached for Cody's throat.

The two men rolled over and over in the sawdust and came up on their knees near the door. Murphy's hands were locked on Cody's neck, and the deputy was gasping for breath. Cody thrust his arms up savagely and broke Murphy's grip. Murphy dove at him, burying his shoulder in Cody's middle as Cody tried to lunge to his feet. Together, they smashed through the batwings onto the boardwalk. Cody's back hit the railing. He felt the wood crack, then he and Murphy were falling into the street. Somewhere nearby, a woman screamed.

Inside the tavern, White Elk saw Cody and Murphy disappear through the door. He was trading punches with one of the other men. He blocked a blow, then crossed a wicked left to his opponent's jaw, peppered three quick punches into the man's midsection, and then hooked a savage right that jerked his head the other way. The man's eyes rolled up in his head, and his legs buckled.

At the same time, Orion caught his opponent in a bear hug. He ignored the blows that the man rained on his back and shoulders and squeezed until his foe gasped, turned red, and went limp. Orion released him and stepped back, and the man collapsed on the floor.

Cody and Murphy were battling outside. White Elk and Orion turned toward the door at the same moment and hurried to make sure the deputy was all right.

In the street, Murphy's punches had Cody staggering, and Murphy's eyes blazed with a mixture of drunken anger and hatred. He knocked Cody backward several steps, and suddenly his hand reached toward the gun on his hip.

The deputy saw the threatening movement and reacted instinctively. His fingers darted toward his Colt, the draw so fast it was almost invisible. Murphy would not stand a chance.

Cody's hand slapped against empty leather. His gun had fallen out sometime during the fracas. It was lying somewhere in the tavern or in the dust of the street, he knew, but the gun's whereabouts were not important now.

Murphy pulled his pistol, jerking the gun up and lining the barrel on Cody.

A shot blasted, but it did not come from Murphy's gun.

Murphy staggered, his mouth drooping open. The gun in his hand sagged toward the ground. It exploded as his trigger finger clenched involuntarily, and a bullet rammed into the dirt. Crimson gurgled from his mouth, and a second later he pitched forward.

Stunned, Cody looked past the dead man at the troop of cavalry sitting on their horses thirty feet away. He had not heard them ride up, but their arrival had undoubtedly saved his life. Smoke curled from the pistol held by a brawny man wearing a campaign hat and sergeant's stripes. Next to the sergeant, mounted on a skittish horse he was struggling to control, a young man in the uniform of a captain snapped, "I told you to fire a warning shot, Drake, not to kill the man."

With a slow smile, the sergeant slid his gun into its holster and snapped the flap shut. "Sorry, Cap'n," he said. "My aim's not as good as it used to be."

White Elk and Orion stood on the boardwalk

staring at the dead man and the cavalry. White Elk's face was taut as he looked at the blue uniforms and recognized some of the men wearing them.

The sound of booted feet pounding on the boardwalk made the deputy turn around. Marshal Luke Travis, his gun in his hand, ran to Cody. "What the devil's going on here?" he demanded. His eyes darted from Cody to Hutch Murphy's dead body to the riders.

Quickly, Cody explained what had happened. As the deputy spoke, the marshal knelt beside Murphy and shook his head when he saw the man was dead.

Drawing a deep breath, White Elk stepped off the boardwalk and walked toward the cavalrymen. He gave a curt nod to the troop's young commanding officer and said brusquely, "Hello, Hogan. Didn't expect to run into you here. I thought I was clear of the Army for a while."

"Duquesne," the captain said.

The sergeant who had shot Murphy grinned arrogantly at White Elk. "Howdy, Kiowa," he said. "Taken any scalps since you've been off the reservation?"

White Elk ignored the contemptuous sergeant. "What are you doing here, Hogan? You must've come a long way."

"A long way indeed," the captain agreed. "And we're here because of you, Duquesne."

White Elk stared in puzzlement, but before he could ask any questions, Travis came over and said to the officer, "Hello, Captain. I'm Luke Travis, the marshal of Abilene, and this is my deputy, Cody

Fisher. Looks like you and your men saved his life."

"I merely saw one man about to shoot another man who was unarmed," Captain Hogan answered stiffly. "I did not intend for anyone to be killed."

Cody had found his pistol lying in the street and scooped it up. Quickly he examined it for dirt and fouling, then slid it into its holster. "Well, Murphy intended to kill me," he said. "I'm much obliged for the help, mister."

"You and your men have business in Abilene, Captain?" Travis asked.

"We certainly do," Hogan replied. He glanced at White Elk. "If we could go to your office, Marshal, I'll explain the whole thing."

"Sure." Travis nodded.

"Why don't you come with us, Duquesne?" Hogan said to the scout.

"I intend to," White Elk replied grimly. Something had to be very wrong for Hogan's troop to have been dispatched all the way up here to search for him.

He began to wonder whether he had simply run into trouble since coming to Abilene—or if he had brought it with him.

On an isolated farm far to the south of Abilene, Wiley Peake and his brother Calvin had been scratching a living from the soil for five long years. It was a lonely existence, but at least they did not have to answer to anyone. They lived their lives the way they saw fit.

At the moment, Wiley would not have minded

working for wages for a change. He had gotten up long before dawn and had been plowing the north field behind a particularly stubborn mule all morning. Now he was on his way to the house for lunch.

Calvin probably would not have anything prepared, Wiley thought gloomily. His brother had been planning to spend the morning fixing the fence around the barn. It was just like Calvin to latch onto an easy job and then expect Wiley to fix their midday meal.

Wiley, a stocky man in his thirties with a week's growth of beard, plodded along. Today was Saturday, or at least he was pretty sure it was. After they had eaten, he and Calvin would scrape off their stubble and head into Caldwell for a few drinks. That would be the highlight of their week; they did not have enough money for a woman this time.

As he approached the ramshackle cabin, Wiley saw that no smoke curled from the chimney. And there was no sign of Calvin at the barn. Maybe he was inside putting away his tools, Wiley thought.

South of the house was a thick stand of trees. Wiley thought he saw a sudden flicker of movement in the shadows there, like a horse tossing its head. But as he frowned and peered more closely, he decided he must have been imagining it; he could see nothing.

His thick-soled shoes clomped as he climbed the steps to the cabin door. He wrenched it open and stepped inside. "Calvin?" he called. "You in here, durn it?"

A moment later, he screamed.

His brother's body lay face down in a pool of blood on the plank floor of the kitchen. Calvin

Peake's skull was crushed, and someone had been working on his body with knives as well. Wiley had never seen so much blood, but it was the flinty red face of the Indian who stood over Calvin that made Wiley shriek in fear.

More Indians grabbed Wiley from behind and forced him forward. Wiley tried to writhe out of their grip until he felt the sharp point of a blade dig into his back and a trickle of blood snake its wet way toward his waist. Then he stared into the fierce, dark eyes of the Indian who stood over Calvin.

"We only need one," the savage abruptly said in English. "You will do, dog of a white man. We will let you live if you can do one thing."

Overcome by fear, Wiley babbled incoherently.

The Indian casually stepped over Calvin's bloody corpse. He raised his hand, and Wiley's eyes fixed on the crimson-stained blade he held. The Indian put the point against Wiley's beard-stubbled throat and said, "I am Buffalo Knife, white man, and you will show me the way to the place called Abilene."

Chapter Six

━━━◆━━━

CAPTAIN JONATHAN HOGAN WAS A TALL YOUNG MAN with a lean face and crisp brown hair. He had been raised in Massachusetts, the son of a well-to-do family, and had attended West Point, graduating in the lower third of his class but still a respectable distance from the bottom. White Elk had known him for a little over a year. During that time, the scout had come to realize that someday Hogan might make a halfway decent soldier, if the frontier did not kill him first. At the moment, though, he was a long way from being a good officer.

As he entered Travis's office, Hogan took off his gloves, folded them, and stuck them behind his belt. Then he removed his hat and tried to knock some of the trail dust from it.

Sergeant Virgil Drake, a burly man with thinning

sandy hair, slouched in behind him. Drake was a veteran noncom and looked it. The Army was the only life he had known since his mid-teens.

White Elk, Travis, and Cody followed the two cavalrymen into the office. Orion had gone to the undertaker's to arrange to have Murphy's body removed. Once that was done, the saloonkeeper would return to the tavern to assess the damage that had been done in the brawl.

Travis flipped his hat onto one of the pegs just inside the door and went behind the desk. He motioned at the chair opposite him. "Have a seat, Captain," he said to Hogan. "You look like a man who has a story to tell."

"It's not a pretty one, I'm afraid," Hogan replied grimly as he sat down. Drake stood behind him, looking bored.

Cody grabbed one of the chairs that sat against the wall and straddled it as he cuffed back his hat. "Thanks again, Sarge," he said to Drake. "That was a pretty good shot."

"Like I told the captain, sir, I guess my aim was off," Drake said. "I was figuring to shoot over the man's head." Everyone in the room heard the mocking insincerity in his voice.

White Elk was not surprised that Drake had shot to kill. The man had learned the lessons of a soldier early and well, and White Elk was convinced that Drake *enjoyed* killing.

Travis leaned back in his chair. "You were saying, Captain?" he prompted.

Hogan nodded and looked closely at White Elk. "Buffalo Knife has escaped," he said slowly.

White Elk gasped, and he felt his heart thudding

in his chest. "How long ago?" he finally managed to ask.

"A little over a week," Hogan replied. "We were out on patrol. Headquarters sent a rider with a dispatch after us. We were told to come here at once to alert you and the local authorities."

Travis straightened and laced his hands together. "Who is this Buffalo Knife?" he asked.

"He's a Kiowa brave. One of their war chiefs, I suppose you would call him."

White Elk added, "I've known him for years, Marshal. We were friends once, when I was still living with my mother's people." He paused, then said in a bleak voice, "That's one reason he wants to kill me now."

"He's got at least a dozen braves with him," Hogan said, "plus any renegades he's managed to pick up since leaving the reservation. General Mackenzie is afraid this is going to be a major murder raid, Duquesne. And you know that you'll be the real object of it."

White Elk nodded. He turned to Travis and Cody, who were staring at him with a mixture of puzzlement and concern. "Buffalo Knife was one of Quanah's right-hand men during the Red River War," he explained. "Like most of the warriors, he was rounded up and placed on a reservation after the fight at Palo Duro Canyon. The last time I saw him, he told me that I was responsible for what had happened to his people. He blames me for their defeat, Marshal. According to him, I've got the blood of scores of brave Kiowas on my hands."

"And now this man's on the loose," Travis

mused. "Sounds bad. But what makes you think he's coming to Abilene, Captain?"

Hogan gestured toward White Elk. "Like Duquesne says, Buffalo Knife hates him and above all else wants to kill him. He didn't hesitate to kill several troopers during his escape. On their way out of the agency, he and his men captured one of the Crow scouts who was staying there."

"Falling Moon!" White Elk exclaimed.

Hogan nodded. "That's right. We found his body a few miles away. He had been severely tortured." The captain looked at White Elk. "Did the Crow know where you were going, Duquesne?"

White Elk nodded slowly. "I told him I was coming to Abilene to try to find my father," he said, his voice harsh. "Falling Moon was a good friend, dammit!"

"But he would have told Buffalo Knife what he wanted to know."

"Yes. I'm afraid you're right. Not many men can stand up under torture for long." White Elk faced Travis. "There's a good chance Buffalo Knife will be heading here, Marshal. But at least we've been warned."

Cody looked dubious. "You really think this Buffalo Knife would raid a town the size of Abilene?"

"To get at me, he probably would," White Elk replied. "He believes he has a blood debt to settle. He'll gladly give up his own life for the chance to kill me."

"That's what General Mackenzie thinks, too," Hogan agreed. He looked at Travis. "I'm to put myself and my men at your disposal, Marshal. We'll stay here in Abilene until Buffalo Knife arrives or is recaptured."

Travis frowned as he digested the information. Then he said, "I've always tried to cooperate with the military, Captain. If there's a chance of Indian trouble, I'm glad you're here. I have one favor to ask of you, though. If the townspeople realize there's a possibility of an Indian raid, they'll panic. I don't want that."

"Neither do I, Marshal. I assure you we'll keep the details of our mission to ourselves."

"Don't you think folks have a right to know if they're in danger, Marshal?" Cody asked.

"Yes," Travis said. "But for the time being, let's keep things quiet. If we hear that Buffalo Knife is getting close to town, we'll have enough time to clear folks out."

White Elk stalked across the room and peered through a window at the street. He saw men, women, and children hurrying by, people who had no idea that soon they might be in mortal danger. To many of Abilene's citizens, Indian trouble was a thing of the past. They might learn differently now, and it would be his fault.

White Elk swung around and faced Travis. "I think I should leave, Marshal," he said flatly. "I don't want to put your people in danger."

Travis pushed back his chair, but before he could say anything, Captain Hogan spoke. "That wouldn't do any good. If Buffalo Knife knows you were heading here, the town is going to be in danger no matter where you are. Having you leave won't help Abilene now."

Travis nodded. "Besides, if he finds out you're on the run, he'll just follow you, and then any folks in his way will be in trouble," he said.

"It's better if you stay here," Hogan said. "That way we can prepare for Buffalo Knife's arrival. With any luck, we can capture him with a minimum of risk to the civilians."

White Elk looked at Travis and Hogan for a long moment, then finally nodded. He knew they were right, and besides, he had never been a man to run from trouble.

"Who knows, Buffalo Knife may be caught before he gets close to Abilene," Hogan said. "Then we'll have worried for nothing."

White Elk thought the captain would be disappointed if that happened. Hogan was probably looking forward to a fight, the scout mused. If the young officer could recapture Buffalo Knife—under dramatic circumstances—he would make a name for himself. White Elk doubted that Hogan would deliberately endanger the town, but he would seize any opportunity to further his career.

Travis shifted his attention from Hogan to Sergeant Drake, who had been standing quietly during the discussion. The marshal said, "Now, Sergeant, there is the matter of that man you killed a few minutes ago."

Drake jerked his sleepy eyes up. "I was just followin' orders, Marshal," he declared. "Ain't my fault I missed."

"I won't argue that point with you," Travis said dryly. "And since you probably saved my deputy's life, I don't think there will be any charges brought against you. However, you will have to attend the inquest and testify before the coroner's jury. You have any problem with that?"

Drake looked at his commanding officer. "What about it, Captain?"

"We always cooperate with local lawmen, Drake," Hogan replied. "The sergeant will be available whenever you need him, Marshal."

Travis nodded. "That's fine."

Hogan stood up, pulled his gloves from his belt, and slapped them against the palm of his other hand. "We'll make camp on the edge of town. Do you have any suggestions for a campsite, Marshal?"

"There's a pretty good field near Mud Creek, on the west side of town," Travis said. "Water's nearby, and there are some shade trees."

Cody got to his feet. "I know the place you mean, Marshal. I can show the troopers where it is."

"Thank you, Deputy," Hogan said as he turned toward the door. He glanced at White Elk. "I'll expect to see you later, Duquesne. We need to make plans for Buffalo Knife."

White Elk hesitated. Hogan was too quick to issue orders. The scout was not under his command at the moment. But he would not accomplish anything by getting upset about it.

"All right," he said. "I'll ride over to your camp once you're settled in."

Hogan nodded and went out, followed by Drake and Cody. Travis watched them go, then said to White Elk, "Looks like that peaceful visit of yours isn't going to turn out that way."

"It hasn't been very peaceful," White Elk replied distractedly. There had already been the trouble with Murphy and his friends; now a much greater threat loomed on the horizon.

A threat that might touch people he had come to care about—like Cody and Orion, Grace Pinkston and Rita Nevins, even his own father . . . and Lora.

The scout's face set in hard lines. He would not allow Lora to come to any harm. Not even if it cost him his life.

Chapter Seven

———◆———

THE NEXT FEW DAYS PASSED QUIETLY. THE DICKINSON County coroner, who was also the local undertaker, held an inquest into the death of Hutch Murphy. Following testimony from White Elk, Cody, Orion, and Sergeant Virgil Drake, the jury determined that the shooting of Murphy was justifiable.

The result surprised no one. Murphy was buried with only the undertaker and Luke Travis in attendance. The man had been a drifter like his friends, and those friends had moved on after Murphy's death. Travis had fined the two who had been part of the brawl in Orion's, but only enough to cover the damages.

The cavalry troop established their camp on the edge of town. Travis and Cody spread the story that the soldiers were awaiting the delivery of a herd of cattle from Texas. The first herds were not expected to come up the trail for several weeks, so the presence of the troop was passed off as bureaucratic inefficiency to those who bothered to ask about it.

Captain Jonathan Hogan, White Elk, and Marshal Travis had conferred at length, devising plans to protect the town. The three men had decided that Hogan would send several small patrols out on a regular basis to check for any signs of approaching Indians. In addition, Travis would keep a close watch on the telegraph traffic. Without telling the Western Union operator what he was looking for, Travis elicited the man's promise to inform him right away of any unusual information coming over the wire. If there were raids anywhere in the state, Travis was certain he would know of them immediately.

That done, all went about their business, giving the appearance that nothing was amiss in Abilene.

Rita and Grace had heard about the brawl and the shooting, and White Elk had had to reassure them repeatedly that he was unhurt. When he visited his father's house again, this time staying for dinner, he worried that Lora would have heard the same story. He did not know what he would tell her if she asked why Murphy had picked a fight. He decided after much thought to use the prejudice against half-breeds as an excuse.

Unless, of course, Lora had heard that the grudge had its origins in the clash at Grace Pinkston's. Then she would probably want to know what he had been doing there in the first place.

He worried needlessly. Lora did not comment on the incident, and White Elk realized that she probably had not heard about it. Given the advanced stage of her pregnancy, he doubted that she left the house very often.

After White Elk had cleared the table for Lora, he joined Pierre in the parlor. Lora discreetly withdrew after a few minutes to leave the men alone to talk.

Pierre lit a cigar, and then said around it, "I hear you had a little trouble the other day."

"Murphy wouldn't let go of his grudge," White Elk replied. "He paid for his stubbornness."

"The man always was a hothead," Pierre grunted.

"Then why did you let him keep coming to the house?"

Pierre shrugged. "His money was as good as anybody else's. Just because I don't like a man doesn't make him a bad customer."

"That's a practical way to look at it," White Elk said with a thin smile.

"I'm a practical man."

White Elk leaned back in his chair and debated whether or not to tell Pierre about the threat from Buffalo Knife. He was confident that Pierre would not say anything about it to Lora or anyone else. His father had his faults, but he was not a gossip. But he decided against it. This was his problem, his and the Army's. If Pierre knew about it, he would only resent his son that much more.

Lora reappeared in the doorway. Her face was pale, and she clutched at the door for support. When White Elk saw her, he stood up quickly and started toward her. "Are you all right?" he asked. He noticed that Pierre had not budged.

Lora smiled. "I'm fine, White Elk," she assured him. "Just a bit tired." Looking past him, she went on, "Pierre, I believe I'll retire for the evening."

Pierre nodded curtly. "Good night," he said.

"Good night, White Elk," Lora added.

"If there's anything I can do . . ." he began.

Lora shook her head. "Don't worry. It's very normal to be tired at a time like this."

He called, "Good night," after her as she went down the hall. When he turned to face his father, he saw Pierre glowering at him.

"You're awfully concerned about my wife's welfare, boy," the older man snapped.

"Somebody's got to be," White Elk replied heatedly. "Can't you see she's not well?"

"She's fine. The only thing wrong with her is that she's going to have a baby, and that's nothing to worry about. Your ma dropped you without any trouble."

"Has Lora seen the doctor recently?"

"Hell, I don't know. I don't see why a woman needs a doctor for something as natural as birthing a baby."

White Elk stared at his father, unable to understand his cavalier attitude toward Lora's health. He decided to visit the doctor's office and introduce himself to Aileen Bloom. He wanted an informed opinion on Lora's condition.

"I think I'll be going," he said, reaching for his hat.

Pierre grinned humorlessly. "Enjoy yourself."

White Elk stood silently for a moment, then wheeled and went to the door. He let himself out and walked into the warm night air, wondering why every visit with his father had to end with bitterness.

Sergeant Virgil Drake grinned broadly as he strode into the parlor of Grace Pinkston's house. An excited corporal and three privates followed him. They had been on the trail a long time before arriving in Abilene, and having to spend several nights in camp while there were women nearby had been almost more than they could stand. At first, Captain Hogan had been his usual stiff-necked self. With the exception of the frequent patrols, he had kept everybody in camp, but at last the grumbling had gotten to be too much even for him, and he issued evening passes.

Drake and the other men did not have to return to the camp until ten o'clock. They intended to use every minute of their free time to the fullest.

The soldiers had begun their evening at the Alamo Saloon, where they had polished off a bottle of whiskey. Once they were relaxed they knew they were ready for something more.

When she first saw the soldiers at her front door, Grace had moved back quickly and opened the door wide to admit them. As she stood in the hall looking at them closely, there was more than a little trepidation on her handsome face. "What can we do for you gentlemen?" she asked.

Drake leered at her. "We ain't gentlemen, and we're here to howl! Bring on the women!"

A half-dozen women were lounging in the parlor. They exchanged quick glances as the soldiers tramped in. The evening had been rather slow, but the arrival of the cavalrymen would change that.

Grace gestured at the waiting women and said, "As you can see, Sergeant, we have several elegant ladies prepared to offer you and your friends the finest companionship. Would you care for some champagne while you make their acquaintance?"

"Yeah, Sarge!" one of the privates said enthusiastically. "Champagne!"

"I guess we could do with a bottle," Drake agreed. Then, rubbing his hands together in anticipation, he strode into the room, his eye already on a buxom redhead.

With a great deal of hilarity, the soldiers moved into the parlor and quickly paired up with the women. Drake fished in his pocket and produced several coins, which he tossed to Grace. "For that champagne," he said as he slipped his arm around the redhead's shoulders and boldly caressed her.

One of the women brought the bottle and glasses, but before she could pour, Drake snatched the bottle from her hand and brought it to his lips. The champagne gurgled loudly in the bottle before he finally lowered it and passed it to one of the other men, who seized it greedily.

Drake returned to nuzzling the neck of the woman beside him on the divan. She giggled and tried halfheartedly to push him away.

The other soldiers were carrying on with the women they had picked out. Grace watched the goings-on with a tired gaze; she had seen plenty of soldiers in her time and knew they were in for a busy night. Malachi appeared in the foyer and raised an eyebrow quizzically when Grace glanced over at him.

"Any trouble, Miz Grace?" the black man asked quietly. "I heard the uproar back in the kitchen."

"Just a few soldiers," Grace replied with a smile. "You know how they are, Malachi."

He nodded his head. "Yes, ma'am, I surely do. You holler if you need help."

"Of course, Malachi."

Malachi cast a dubious glance at the celebrating troopers and ambled back to the kitchen.

Within minutes, the bottle of champagne was empty, and Drake was shouting for a fresh one. After a nod from Grace, a girl hurried to fetch it.

Two of the cavalrymen began singing a bawdy song. The women with them soon picked up the lyrics and joined in. Drake leaned back against the divan, his arms full of perfumed flesh, and savored the hot, wet taste of the redhead's mouth. A night like this made up for all the miserable conditions of the job. Even serving under an officer like Hogan did not seem so bad at the moment.

Those thoughts were running through Drake's head as he broke the kiss and said, "Abilene ain't such a bad place. Wouldn't mind stayin' here awhile."

The redhead snuggled closer. "Well, why can't you, sweetie? You can stay as long as you want, as far as I'm concerned."

"Hell, in a few days we'll either be dead or have orders to head somewhere else."

The prostitute pulled away and frowned at him. "Dead? What are you talking about?"

Drake tried to focus on her painted face. "That damn Injun won't stop with Duquesne. He'll try to kill us all, wipe out the whole town more'n likely."

The prostitute's fingers tightened on his shoulders. "Oh, my God!" she whispered. "Indians are coming here?"

Drake nodded solemnly, forgetting his orders to keep quiet about the danger in his desire to impress the redhead. "That's right," he declared. "Band of murderin' renegades led by Buffalo Knife. The captain figures they're headin' for Abilene to kill that half-breed skunk, White Elk."

The woman suddenly twisted out of his arms and stood up shakily. "Grace!" she cried out, turning toward the madam's chair. "Grace!"

The madam hurried over, a concerned look on her face. The other women glanced anxiously at the redhead, although the soldiers were oblivious to her dismay. Grace caught her arm and said, "What's wrong, Phoebe?"

The woman leveled a finger at the smirking Drake and began, "He says we're all going to be—"

Suddenly realizing what he had done, Drake surged to his feet and gripped her shoulder to silence her. He shook his head as if to clear the fog of whiskey and champagne in his brain. "I didn't say nothin'," he snapped. "Not a damn thing."

Grace stared at the sergeant, well aware that something was wrong. But she did not want to upset the other girls. Quickly, she said to the redhead, "You can tell me all about it later, Phoebe. Maybe right now you'd like to go upstairs for a little bit, since you're upset."

"She's with me," Drake rumbled. "She ain't goin' upstairs unless I go with her."

Grace turned to him and said, "Sergeant, the girl

is upset. There are many other young ladies here who can show you a good time."

Drake's face set in truculent lines. He was going to be stubborn. He wished he had not let it slip about the Indian threat, but he would not let that mistake rob him of his evening's pleasure.

"Please, mister," Phoebe implored as she clutched at Drake's arm. She was biting her lower lip and obviously making an effort to restrain her fright. "I wouldn't be much good for you right now."

"Well . . ." Drake said, rubbing his jaw.

A flurry of movement in the parlor doorway interrupted the trio. Phoebe's eyes lit up when she glanced over and saw Rita coming into the room. "There's the girl you want!" she exclaimed, nodding toward the lovely strawberry blonde. She ignored Grace, who was urgently shaking her head.

Drake turned toward Rita and caught his breath as he saw how beautiful she was. All the women in this bordello were attractive, but Rita was exceptionally so. She stopped just inside the parlor, feeling Drake's hungry stare.

"Yeah," Drake breathed. "I think you're right, Phoebe-gal."

Grace moved between Drake and Rita. "I'm afraid that's impossible," she said. "Rita's not working with the regular customers anymore—"

"Why not, Grace?" Phoebe hissed angrily. "Is she too good to be a whore now that she's been with White Elk?"

"She's Duquesne's girl?" Drake asked eagerly before Grace could answer Phoebe's question.

Phoebe turned toward him. "That's right. The

way they've been acting, you'd think she was his property."

Drake reached into his tunic, drew out a roll of bills, and thrust them at Grace. "I want her," he said simply.

Grace stared at the money in his outstretched hand. A few feet away, Rita stood stiffly, her green eyes staring nervously at Grace. The discussion had also drawn the attention of the other soldiers, who stopped pawing the prostitutes to watch the confrontation.

Grace bit her lower lip. Looking at the expressions Drake and his companions wore, she believed that the troopers might go crazy and tear the place up if she refused their sergeant's request. Besides, it was not as if Rita had been a blushing virgin before White Elk arrived in Abilene. She was a prostitute and had been used by hundreds of men. What difference would one more make?

"All right," Grace said abruptly. She reached out and took the money from Drake's hand.

"Grace . . ." Rita said, her voice low, pleading.

The madam spun around. "You go with this gentleman, and you treat him nice, you hear?" she said sharply.

Rita stared at her for a long moment, anger glittering in her eyes. Finally, she said, "I hear." She stood still as Drake stepped forward and took her arm.

"We're goin' right upstairs," the sergeant declared. "I've had enough liquor for tonight."

"Sure, soldier," Rita said, nodding numbly. She did not resist as Drake led her out of the parlor to the staircase. Grace watched them go with a worried look on her face. She wished there had been some other way out of this dilemma, but she had done what she had to do. The other troopers had gone back to their women and drinks; maybe now the evening could pass without a brawl.

Still tightly grasping Rita's arm, Drake panted in anticipation as he climbed the stairs. It was obvious that there was something between this girl and White Elk, which made the prospect of bedding her that much more appealing. Word of what he was doing would certainly get back to Duquesne. The half-breed scout would be furious when he learned what had happened.

At least Drake hoped so. If White Elk was mad enough, he might come looking for trouble, and Drake would be glad to oblige him. He had never liked the half-breed or the way he associated with white folks, as if he was as good as they were. White Elk Duquesne was just another redskin as far as Sergeant Virgil Drake was concerned. And Drake firmly believed in the old adage that the only good Indian was a dead one.

Rita led him down the second-floor hall to the last room. Her face was an expressionless mask as she opened the door and stepped inside. Drake followed her, looked around, and grunted, "Nice place. 'Course, I'm payin' enough for the privilege of usin' it."

"Let's get this over with," Rita said flatly.

He put a hand on her shoulder and spun her around to face him. "The woman downstairs told you to treat me nice, remember? You ain't soundin' too happy about this."

Rita forced a professional smile onto her lips. "Sorry," she murmured.

Drake's fingers tightened on her flesh. "You're just upset because I ain't that redskin who's been beddin' you. Hell, you'll find out I'm a whole lot better than he ever could be."

"I'm sure," Rita said coolly.

Drake heard the insincerity in her voice. With a snarl, he yanked her roughly against him and brought his mouth down on hers.

Rita tried to twist away, but Drake's arms went around her and held her tightly. She let out a cry as she pulled her head away and struggled against his brutal embrace.

"Dammit, quit fightin'!" Drake rasped. "I don't mind a little, but I'm tired of this, gal." His blunt, calloused fingers caught the neck of her gown and abruptly ripped down. Drake shoved her toward the bed, and as the back of her knees hit the mattress, she fell. The sergeant loomed over her, pulling and tearing at her gown, baring her breasts. She balled her fists and struck at his face.

One of the blows connected, but only glanced off and enraged him further. His hand whipped across her face in a ringing slap that jerked her head to the side. "You damn slut!" he snarled. He ripped the rest of her torn gown off, leaving her naked and struggling on the bed. "I'll teach you a lesson, you hellcat!"

He slapped her again, twice, the sharp crack of flesh against flesh filling the room.

Rita screamed.

* * *

White Elk was still in a bad mood as he rode toward Grace's house. He was worried about Lora, about her condition, and about his father's lack of concern. Having a baby was a natural event, but White Elk knew of women who had died in childbirth. He did not want that to happen to Lora. He told himself once more that he would see Dr. Aileen Bloom tomorrow to learn how Lora was really doing.

He swung his horse into the drive and walked the animal to the stable behind the house. No one questioned his movements now. After nearly a week in Abilene, he supposed he had become a fixture.

White Elk unsaddled his horse, checked that the animal had grain and water, and went to the back door of the house. He stepped into the kitchen and found Malachi working at the stove. The black man looked up with an expression of concern on his face.

"Hello, Mr. Duquesne," Malachi said quickly. "How was your dinner?"

White Elk grinned. "My father is as endearing as ever, Malachi. I imagine that answers your question."

"Indeed it does, sir." Malachi moved forward to block White Elk's way as the scout started toward the hall. "Miz Grace would like to see you whenever it's convenient."

"In a few minutes," White Elk nodded. "I want to let Rita know that I'm back. Is she in the parlor?"

"Ah, no, I don't think she is, Mr. Duquesne." Malachi seemed nervous about something, White

Elk thought. That impression was confirmed as the black man went on hurriedly, "Don't you think you should go see Miz Grace right now, sir? She's waiting in her office."

White Elk shrugged. "All right, I'll talk to her. Just let me go to the parlor first. I could use a drink."

"I'll get that for you, sir," Malachi offered.

White Elk frowned at him. "What's going on here, Malachi? Why don't you want me to go into the parlor?"

"Well, sir, I was just trying to be polite—"

"Thanks," White Elk cut in. "I appreciate it. But I'll get my own drink." He strode past Malachi and headed down the hall.

He heard Grace pop out of her office a moment after he passed her door. She called his name, but he did not stop. By now, his curiosity demanded that he get to the bottom of this strange behavior.

He could hear excited chattering coming from the parlor. When he stepped into the room, everyone suddenly stopped speaking. Four troopers were sitting around the room with women on their laps. Several young women were clustered around the redhead called Phoebe. Phoebe stared at him for a long moment, then lifted a hand and pointed. "It's him!" she said in a shaky voice. "Him that's going to be the death of us all!"

A chill traveled up White Elk's spine. "What's happened here?" he demanded.

The corporal replied. "The sarge had a little too much to drink and let the news about Buffalo Knife slip, Duquesne. These gals are gettin' all worked up about it." He slapped the bare thigh of the prostitute perched on his lap. " 'Course, worked up is the way we want 'em, ain't it, boys?"

White Elk uttered a heartfelt curse. Drake had done the very thing that Marshal Travis and Captain Hogan had wanted to avoid. Now that these women knew about Buffalo Knife, the entire town would be up in arms before the next sunset.

"Where is Drake?" White Elk asked grimly.

"He's upstairs with your private whore!" Phoebe spat at him.

Suddenly the chill in White Elk spread, until it gripped his very soul. "Rita?" he asked in a tight voice.

"That's right," Phoebe shot back. "They went up a few minutes ago."

White Elk spun around to find Grace standing behind him. He glared at her, but she met his gaze levelly and stood fixed in his path. "Wait a minute, White Elk," the madam said firmly. "This is a business."

"Get out of my way," he said quietly.

"I'll call Malachi," Grace warned.

Her words of caution meant nothing to him. White Elk pushed past Grace, who gasped in surprise but did not call for Malachi. Instead, White Elk vaguely heard her saying angrily, "I thought you were going upstairs to rest, Phoebe. Well, you'll have plenty of time for that now. You're through!"

White Elk found Malachi waiting beside the stairs. That was why Grace had not called him. "You'd best not go up there, Mr. Duquesne," the black man said.

"I don't want to fight you, Malachi," White Elk

said as the black man moved smoothly to block the stairs. "But I will if I have to."

Malachi started to speak when a frightened scream came from upstairs. White Elk's head jerked up, and he cried, "Rita!"

Malachi turned to gaze in surprise up the stairs, and White Elk bounded past him before the black man could stop him. White Elk took the stairs two at a time. He heard Malachi pounding after him, but he did not turn around or slow down.

When he reached the second-floor hallway, he raced down the corridor toward the last door. As he approached it, he heard muffled grunts and curses, punctuated by the sound of a slap. White Elk threw himself against the door.

It gave slightly, and he pulled back and slammed into it again. This time the latch tore out of the jamb, and the door flew open. As his eyes took in the scene, White Elk staggered into the room, trying to catch his balance.

Rita was sprawled on the bed, her gown in tatters around her. Looming above her was the bulky figure of Sergeant Virgil Drake. Drake was trying to pull off his shirt with one hand while he used the other to hold down the struggling Rita. He was looking over his shoulder with an angry snarl.

"Drake!" White Elk cried. Enraged, he sprang at the sergeant, grabbed his shoulder, and jerked him away from Rita. Blind rage gave him the strength to fling his larger opponent toward the wall. Swinging viciously, White Elk lunged after Drake.

Drake hit the wall and rebounded into White Elk's fist. Before the sergeant could recover, White Elk lowered his shoulder, tackled Drake, and forced the heavy man toward the door. He heard Rita crying his name from somewhere far away.

Drake clasped his hands together and brought the clubbed fists down on White Elk's back. The blow loosened White Elk's grip, and Drake twisted away. Panting, he swung a punch at White Elk's head.

Slipping to the side to avoid the blow, White Elk saw Malachi behind Drake. The black man stood with his fists balled, ready to leap into the fight. The scout darted backward, away from another of Drake's sweeping punches, and shook his head. "The bastard's mine!" he gasped to the black man.

Malachi stepped away with a grin tugging at his mouth.

Drake lunged at White Elk, his face contorted in anger. White Elk dodged desperately. He had been able to tackle Drake in the early stages of the fight because the sergeant had been taken by surprise and was off-balance. But all that had changed, and the big man was now fighting with everything that he had. White Elk knew that he must not let Drake get his arms around him: the big man's superior weight and strength would destroy him. Now, White Elk had to rely on his speed and cunning.

He snapped a couple of quick, stinging punches at Drake's midsection. Drake howled and flung a pair of punches that would have ended the fight had they connected. White Elk avoided them easily, dancing around Drake and drawing the berserk sergeant away toward the stairs.

White Elk caught a glimpse of Rita as she appeared in the doorway, a sheet wrapped around her nakedness. Anxious lines were etched on her lovely face as she watched the two men battle. He did not want her to be hurt accidentally, so the farther away he could draw Drake, the better.

He kept peppering Drake with punches, taking a few in return but managing to make Drake miss with most of them. The blows that did connect staggered White Elk, and he knew that he could not take too much of that kind of punishment.

He was aware that the staircase was close behind him now. Shouts of encouragement came from the crowd of people at the bottom of the stairs. The troopers were calling for Drake to defeat him, but Malachi and most of the prostitutes were on his side.

White Elk jabbed at Drake's face and felt the crunch of cartilage as the fist slammed the sergeant's nose. Blood splattered over White Elk's knuckles. Drake bellowed in pain and charged blindly.

White Elk had been waiting for that. He threw himself to the side and let Drake thunder past him. The sergeant had not noticed that White Elk had reached the very top of the stairs. Drake's feet went out from under him, and he toppled like a tree.

Luck turned against White Elk. One of Drake's flailing hands caught the collar of White Elk's buckskin shirt, and the scout found himself falling right behind Drake.

The two men tumbled head over heels down the stairs. White Elk was jarred, but he managed to avoid hitting his head as he fell. Halfway down, his ribs smashed painfully into a runner, and a moment later he was sprawling atop Virgil Drake's moaning figure.

"He's killed the sarge!" one of the privates shouted. "Get the redskinned son of a bitch!"

The troopers surged forward, grabbed White Elk, and jerked the dazed scout to his feet. Several of the prostitutes pleaded with them to stop, but the soldiers ignored them.

Malachi leaped in and swung a fist at one of the cavalrymen. The man staggered backward from the blow, but three men still hung on to White Elk. One of the troopers released the scout, stepped in front of him, and smashed a blow into his midsection. White Elk gasped and started to buckle over, but the men holding him yanked him upright.

Shaking his head, Drake pushed himself to his feet. He saw his men holding White Elk and pushed aside the man who was about to deliver another brutal blow. With a savage snarl, Drake swung his own fist, driving it into White Elk's unprotected belly. The man Drake had displaced turned to help his companion with Malachi.

It was a full-fledged brawl, the second one in this house in less than a week. In the first one, White Elk and Malachi had been assisted by Pierre Duquesne's timely intervention. Unless something similar happened now, White Elk thought fuzzily as more blows thudded against his body, this fight was going to end differently. Unless somebody stopped him, Virgil Drake was going to beat him to death.

The front door suddenly flew open, and a strong, commanding voice boomed, "Hold it!"

Ignoring the order to stop, Drake continued to hammer White Elk's body with his fists. White Elk saw the tall, imposing figure of Luke Travis appear behind the sergeant's shoulder. Travis whipped the gun in his hand around and slammed the barrel into the back of Drake's head. Drake sagged against White Elk and slid to the floor.

Leveling his Colt at the other troopers, the marshal cocked the gun. "You men back off," he said coldly.

The men holding White Elk did as they were told, and the scout clutched at the wall to keep from falling. Behind Travis he saw Cody Fisher, holding a gun on the two men who had been fighting with Malachi.

"What the devil's going on here?" Travis demanded. "We were taking a turn around town and could hear this ruckus two blocks away!"

Grace Pinkston stepped from the group of cowering prostitutes. "I'm afraid it's my fault, Marshal," she said. She looked meaningfully at White Elk. "I made a mistake in judgment. I never should have allowed these soldiers into the place."

White Elk tried to catch his breath. At least Grace was not blaming him for the fight. He glanced up and saw a worried-looking Rita standing at the top of the stairs. He tried to grin reassuringly, but a sudden pain shot through his chest, and he could not help flinching. As he tried to breathe more shallowly, he wondered if some of his ribs were broken.

Travis looked sternly at Grace. "You know the law doesn't like to bother these houses as long as things are kept peaceful, Mrs. Pinkston. But I've heard that this wasn't the first free-for-all you've had lately."

Moving carefully, White Elk stepped forward. "I

was involved in both of the fights, Marshal," he said, "and I can tell you that neither of them was Grace's fault. If anything, I was to blame."

Cody spoke. "Looks like the soldiers ganged up on you, White Elk."

"He tried to kill the sarge!" one of the troopers protested.

Rita called down from the top of the stairs, "Only because the sergeant was hurting me! Marshal, White Elk was just trying to help me."

Travis nodded thoughtfully. "All right," he said after a moment. "You boys have caused enough trouble for one night. I think a little time in jail will give you a chance to settle down."

"Jail! We can't go to jail, Marshal. We've got to be back in camp by ten!"

Cody grinned. "I'd be glad to ride out and let Captain Hogan know why some of his men won't be reporting back on time, Marshal."

"Later. Let's get these men behind bars first," Travis said. He turned to the troopers and gestured with his gun. "Pick up your sergeant and carry him over to the jail. Get moving."

Grumbling, the troopers picked Drake up and hauled him onto the porch. Travis and Cody, still holding their guns, followed closely behind. White Elk came out and took Travis to one side.

"There's something you'd better know, Marshal," the scout said in a low voice. "Drake shot his mouth off about Buffalo Knife raiding Abilene."

Travis's lean face tightened. "I was hoping that wouldn't happen," he said slowly.

"I know. I'm sorry."

Travis turned to Cody and said, "Take those troopers to the jail." Then he looked at White Elk and gestured toward the house. "Did those women hear Drake?"

White Elk nodded. "I suppose you could ask them to keep quiet about it, but I'm not sure how much good that would do."

"Probably not much," Travis said. "I knew there was a chance one of the soldiers would say something, but I didn't think it would happen this soon. At least I was hoping it wouldn't." The marshal sighed heavily. "Maybe we're worrying about nothing. There haven't been any Indian raids reported so far. Who knows, maybe Buffalo Knife decided to head for Canada instead of coming after you."

"Maybe," White Elk grunted, but he did not believe it for a second.

"Don't worry, we'll keep the town as calm as possible," Travis assured him. He clapped a hand on White Elk's back.

The scout paled and gritted his teeth as the friendly gesture sent jolts of pain spurting through his body. Travis noticed the reaction and frowned.

"You got banged up in that fight more than you're letting on, didn't you?" he asked.

"Drake and I fell down the stairs," White Elk admitted. "I hit my side pretty hard. May have cracked some ribs; I'm not sure."

Travis studied him for a moment, then said, "Come on. I'll take you to Aileen Bloom's. You're lucky you got hurt in Abilene; you won't find a better doctor in the state."

"I don't need a doctor," White Elk protested.

Travis put a hand on his arm. "I figured you'd say that since you're used to taking care of yourself. But if you're really hurt, there's no reason not to get it taken care of. We want you in good shape."

"For Buffalo Knife . . . when he gets here."

Travis looked at him for a long moment, then finally nodded. "That's right," he said.

Chapter Eight

ALTHOUGH HE CONTINUED TO PROTEST THAT HE DID not need medical attention, White Elk walked to Dr. Aileen Bloom's office with the marshal. His injury prevented him from moving too quickly, and Travis slowed his usual brisk pace.

As they walked, Travis asked, "Why don't you tell me what that fight was really all about?"

"You heard," White Elk replied. "Drake was hurting Rita."

"It's none of my business, but that woman isn't just another soiled dove as far as you're concerned."

"That's right," White Elk said.

"And this wasn't the first time you and Drake have had trouble. Am I right?"

For a long moment, White Elk was silent. Finally, he said, "A man like me runs into a lot of people who are bothered by the fact that my mother was an Indian. Drake's one of those folks. We've had run-ins before, but never anything like tonight. I think he would have killed me."

"That's what it looked like to me," Travis said. "I figured I'd better stop him any way I could."

White Elk grinned. "You gave him a pretty good clout on the head."

"Drake'll have a headache when he wakes up, but there shouldn't be any permanent damage."

"Not with his hard skull," White Elk agreed.

Now they had reached Texas Street. Light spilled onto the boardwalk through the batwings of Orion's Tavern, along with loud talk and laughter. The burly Scotsman was doing a good business this evening. As they passed in front of the door, Travis waved to Orion, who stood behind the bar.

Next door, at Dr. Bloom's office, they noticed that a small light was burning inside. "Looks like Aileen's still here," Travis commented. "That's good; saves us the trouble of finding her."

They turned up the walk and stepped onto the porch. Travis knocked on the front door. A moment later, it swung open, and a smiling young woman greeted them. "Why, hello, Luke. How are you?" she said.

Travis swept off his hat and nodded. "I'm fine, Aileen, but my friend is a little bruised. Can you take a look at him?"

"Of course," Aileen Bloom said quickly. "Come in, please."

146

White Elk stepped into the house, and Travis followed right behind him. The lamp in the office lit the foyer as well, and White Elk saw that the doctor was younger than he had first thought. Prettier, too. Aileen Bloom was perhaps thirty years old, and the brunette hair that framed her high-cheekboned face was thick and lustrous.

Aileen stepped into the office, where a medical journal lay open on her desk, picked up the lamp, and carried it to the foyer. "Follow me, please," she said, leading the way down the hall toward the rear of the house.

She ushered White Elk and Travis into a long, narrow room. An examining table stood against one wall, and a tall, glass-fronted cabinet containing bandages, splints, bottles of antiseptic, and vials of medicine was opposite it.

"Luke, help him onto the table, please," Aileen said. She took a white jacket from the peg that hung on the back of the door and slipped it on over her simple cotton dress. "Now, what seems to be the problem?"

"I tumbled down some stairs, ma'am," White Elk explained. "When I move wrong or breathe too deeply, my side hurts quite a bit."

Aileen frowned. "That sounds serious. By the way, I'm Dr. Aileen Bloom."

"This is White Elk Duquesne," Travis said.

Aileen looked up, her eyes narrowed. "Any relation to Pierre and Lora Duquesne?" she asked.

"Pierre is my father," White Elk answered. "Why?"

Aileen shook her head and said, "Nothing, just

curious. Please try to take your shirt off, Mr. Duquesne."

Slowly, White Elk began peeling the buckskin shirt over his head. He grimaced several times as pain coursed through him. When he had the shirt off, he glanced at his torso and winced at the large, vivid bruise that covered his ribs.

Travis whistled softly. "You sure took a licking," he said. "But you're in good hands. I think I'd better go to the jail and make sure that Cody got there with those troopers. He probably did; I haven't heard any shooting."

"There were four of them," White Elk pointed out. "Five if you count Drake. They may have tried to jump him."

Travis laughed. "We'd have heard the uproar. Take good care of him, Aileen."

"Of course," she said with a smile. "Can you lift your arm, Mr. Duquesne?"

White Elk tried to raise his arm as Travis nodded and slipped out of the room. The scout had to stop when his hand was level with his shoulder.

"That hurts?" Aileen asked.

"A bit," he said, frowning.

Her eyes narrowed as she carefully assessed the bruise. Then, with practiced, searching fingers, she probed his side. He gasped sharply. She looked into his eyes, smiled sympathetically, and said. "I'm sorry if this hurts, but I must find out how badly your ribs have been damaged. This is the only way."

"Go right ahead," White Elk told her as he smiled weakly.

* * *

When Travis reached the marshal's office and jail, he found that Cody had locked the five troopers in two of the cells. Through the open cellblock door, he could hear Virgil Drake raving. Cody was seated behind the desk and grinned at the marshal.

"Drake woke up," the deputy said.

"So I hear." Travis returned Cody's wry grin. "You have any problems with them?"

Cody shook his head. "No. I guess they figured if Captain Hogan heard about it, they'd be in more trouble than they could handle." He pushed back his chair and stood up. "I'll ride out there now and tell Hogan."

"Good." Travis took off his hat and hung it on one of the pegs. He left his gun belt on as he went to pick up the coffeepot that was staying warm on the stove. "Don't tell Hogan why we jailed them. Let me handle that."

Cody nodded and left the office, and a moment later Travis heard the deputy's horse galloping out of town. Travis filled his coffee cup, then strolled to the cellblock.

Drake was pacing around the cell that he shared with the corporal. The three privates occupied the next cell. When Drake saw Travis, he flung himself at the cell door, gripped the bars, and thrust his snarling face against them.

"You can't do this, dammit!" he exclaimed. "We're soldiers! You ain't got no jurisdiction over us! You had no right to damn near bust my head open!"

Travis sipped his coffee, then pointed to the badge on his chest. "This says you're wrong, Drake. Anything that happens in my town is my business."

"That's nothing but a goddamn piece of tin! You wait till the cap'n hears about this. You can't lock up the Army!"

Travis shook his head and walked into the office. There was no point in arguing with a man like Drake.

Within a few minutes, Drake quieted down, evidently bored with his own ranting and raving. Travis sat at his desk and spent a peaceful half hour drinking his coffee.

When several horses cantered up outside, Travis knew that Cody had returned and brought company with him. At the sound of bootheels ringing on the boardwalk planks, the marshal stood up. The door opened and Cody came in, followed closely by Captain Jonathan Hogan.

Hogan wore an angry scowl on his face. Even though his uniform was in perfect order, he looked faintly rumpled, as though he had retired before Cody arrived with the news of the arrests. A sleepy-looking corporal stood behind him.

The cavalry officer strode across the office to Travis's desk and glowered at the lawman. Without preamble, he snapped, "What's all this about you locking up some of my men, Marshal?"

Before Travis could answer, Drake called from the cellblock, "That you, Cap'n? You got to get us out of here, sir! That lawdog's crazy!"

Travis gestured toward the cellblock. "I've got Sergeant Drake and four of your men back there, Captain. I'm charging them with assault and disturbing the peace, maybe more."

"What did they do?" Hogan asked tightly. "Your

deputy would only tell me that they had been locked up."

"They were involved in a brawl here in town."

"In one of the saloons?"

Travis shook his head. "In a house owned by a lady named Grace Pinkston."

Hogan's lip curled contemptuously. "In a whore-house, you mean."

"Some would call it that." Travis shrugged.

"You can't be serious. You threw my men in jail because of some scuffle in a bordello?"

"It was more than that," Travis said. "White Elk Duquesne was involved, too. From the looks of it, Drake and the others tried to kill him."

"I don't believe it," Hogan declared flatly. "Sergeant Drake is a good soldier. He would not have tried to hurt Duquesne."

"There are a lot of folks who would disagree," Cody put in. "Besides, Drake was trying to molest one of the women. That's what started it."

Hogan sneered. "That's ridiculous, Deputy. To be blunt, how can you molest a prostitute? That's what they get paid for, isn't it?"

"Not for being slapped around," Travis replied. He moved from behind the desk. "Look, Captain, we've got enough on our plates without worrying about something like this. Why don't we strike a bargain?"

"And what might that be?" Hogan asked stiffly.

"You put Grace Pinkston's place off-limits to your men, and I'll see that there are no charges brought against Drake and his friends."

Hogan considered for a long moment, then finally nodded. "All right," he said. "I don't particularly want my men frequenting bordellos, anyway."

"And Drake and the others spend the night in jail. They need to sleep off all the liquor they put away tonight."

Hogan hesitated, but Travis refused to back down. Grudgingly, Hogan said, "If you really think that's necessary, Marshal, I won't dispute the point. I want to see them, though."

Travis waved a hand at the cellblock door. "Be my guest, Captain."

Hogan strode into the cellblock, holding his gloves in one hand and slapping them against the palm of the other in his habitual gesture. The five troopers in the cells crowded against the bars, and Drake said eagerly, "Howdy, Cap'n. You come to get us out, right?"

"No, I've come to find out why you disobeyed a direct order, Sergeant," Hogan said. "I told you that you could come into town if you wouldn't cause any trouble with the local citizens. Now I find that you've started a fight and damaged a business establishment."

"Hell, Cap'n, it was just a whorehouse!" Drake protested. His tone grew petulant as he went on, "Besides, it was that damned redskin's fault."

"I know you and Duquesne aren't friends, Drake, but that's no excuse to gang up on him." Hogan nodded curtly. "The marshal and I have agreed that you will spend the night in jail. Let it be a lesson to you."

Drake and the troopers exclaimed angrily, but the captain cut them off with a shake of his head.

"You'll be released in the morning . . . if you

don't cause any more trouble tonight," Hogan went on. He glanced at Travis, who was standing in the cellblock doorway. "Isn't that right, Marshal?"

Travis nodded. "That was the agreement. I'll talk to Duquesne and Mrs. Pinkston and ask them not to press charges. I'm sure they'll agree."

"Very well." Hogan turned to stare coldly at Drake and the others. "I'll expect you men to report to me at camp tomorrow morning as soon as you're released. There may well be some other punishment for this little escapade." He strode out of the cellblock without another word.

Travis followed him. "Thanks for going along with me, Captain," he said.

Hogan sighed. "You were right, Marshal. Those men have to be taught a lesson. Drake is a good soldier, but I suppose he can be a bit of a trouble-maker at times."

Cody started to comment on Hogan's under-statement, but Travis caught the deputy's eye and shook his head. "I'll see that they're released first thing in the morning," he promised.

"Very well. I'm sorry this happened, Travis."

"So am I. Good night, Captain."

Hogan nodded and stalked out, his aide trailing him.

Travis stepped onto the boardwalk as Hogan and the corporal were mounting up. "By the way, Captain, have you received any reports on Buffalo Knife?"

Hogan settled himself in his saddle and shook his head. "Not recently. I did receive a dispatch from headquarters saying that a Kansas settler living near the Indian Territory border had been murdered, apparently by renegades. The man's brother was missing and presumed dead as well. But that was the last sign of Buffalo Knife. I'm sure we'll hear from him again, sooner or later."

"I'm afraid you're right," Travis agreed.

Hogan lifted a hand and started to salute out of habit, then turned the gesture into a wave. He and the corporal rode down Texas Street toward the encampment on the edge of town.

Cody joined Travis on the boardwalk. The deputy looked out at the quiet town. The saloons were still brightly lit, but at this hour most of Abilene was sleeping. Cody said, "I don't much like this waiting. If that Indian's going to show up, I'd just as soon he'd hurry up and get it over with."

Travis nodded. "Maybe that's just the way Buffalo Knife wants us to feel."

"You're going to be pretty stiff and sore for a few days, Mr. Duquesne," Aileen Bloom said. "But you were lucky. None of your ribs are broken, as far as I can tell, but you do have some severe bruises."

"I can live with that," White Elk grunted.

Aileen turned from the examining table and went to the cabinet. "I'm going to tape your ribs. That will keep you from straining the muscles around them, and it should relieve the pain."

White Elk nodded. Aileen's competence and professionalism during the examination had impressed him. His confidence in her ability made it easier for him to ask about Lora.

"You mentioned my father and stepmother earlier, Doctor," he began. "Are you treating my stepmother for her, ah, condition?"

Aileen smiled as she took a wide roll of tape and a small pair of scissors from the cabinet. "You make pregnancy sound like a disease that needs a cure, Mr. Duquesne. But I know what you're trying to say, and yes, I am tending to Lora's health. At least I was."

"Was?" White Elk echoed.

Aileen's expression grew serious. "She's stopped coming to see me. I gathered from some of the things she said that her husband was opposed to her seeking medical attention."

"That sounds like my father," White Elk agreed grimly. "He told me that a woman doesn't need a doctor to have a baby. My mother didn't have a doctor when I was born, of course, and he's convinced that's the way it should be."

Aileen shook her head. "I hope you don't mind my saying so, Mr. Duquesne, but that's an absolutely ridiculous attitude. There are so many things that can go wrong during childbirth that it is only common sense to take as many precautions as possible."

"I couldn't agree with you more, Doctor. But it's hard to talk sense to Pierre Duquesne."

Aileen told White Elk to lift his arms again, and she began winding the tape around his torso, pulling it tight to hold the bruised muscles in place. As she worked, she said, "Lora may have a difficult time during delivery. Since this is her first child, and she is small, she may have problems from that alone. If anything else comes up, if the baby is in a breech position . . ." Her voice trailed off as she cinched the tape tightly around White Elk's middle.

The doctor's frank speech embarrassed the scout. He was not accustomed to discussing such things with ladies. Having this beautiful young woman ministering to his bruised body was distraction enough. He said, "You're saying that having this baby could be dangerous for Lora?"

"Yes," Aileen nodded. "That's exactly what I'm saying. Even with a doctor in attendance, she could have problems. It's essential that I be summoned as soon as she goes into labor. The very moment, in fact. Do you understand, Mr. Duquesne?" She finished her taping, stepped back, and gazed at him intently.

"Why are you telling me this?" he asked after a moment. "It's really none of my business."

"We're talking about your stepmother and a little brother or sister for you, Mr. Duquesne. You appear to be the kind of man who would care about things like that."

He hesitated, then finally said, "I suppose that's true. Lora made me feel welcome. I'm very fond of her. I don't want to see anything happen to her."

"Could you possibly speak to your father?"

A grin stretched across the scout's face. "I tried that, Doctor, and it was a waste of time. I think Pierre really cares for Lora, but once he gets an idea in his head, it's almost impossible to change it. He thinks Lora doesn't need your services."

"He's wrong."

"I know." White Elk nodded. "I suppose I can keep an eye on things. Pierre won't like it if I call you when the time comes, but I won't let him stop me."

"Thank you, Mr. Duquesne. That's what I was hoping you would say." Aileen picked up his buckskin shirt. "Here, let me help you with this."

When he had dressed, he settled his bill and then picked up his hat. He winced as he raised his arm to put it on his head. "You were right," he said. "I am sore."

"I don't think the pain will be too bad now that those ribs are taped. If it is, come in, and I'll give you something to ease it."

"Thanks."

"Don't try to do too much for the next few days. Are you staying with your father and stepmother?"

White Elk shook his head. "I've got a room of my own," he said, which was almost true.

"Well, be careful. It would be good if you can find someone to help you."

White Elk thought about Rita. She would probably be happy to fetch and carry for him for a few days. Of course, his injury would cut down on some of their other activities. He would just have to suffer through it.

"Thanks again," he said as he left the doctor's office. He tipped his hat to Aileen, then started toward Grace Pinkston's.

He was crossing Texas Street when Luke Travis hailed him from the opposite boardwalk. Travis strolled into the street to meet him.

"I was just taking my last turn around town for the night," the marshal explained. "What did Aileen find?"

"A bad bruise, but nothing broken," White Elk said. "Has the captain come in for his men yet?"

"He's been and gone, but he didn't take those troopers with him. They're spending the night in jail."

White Elk frowned in surprise. "Hogan agreed to that?"

"He didn't have much choice." Travis grinned. "I figured Drake and the others needed to sleep it off. I told Hogan that you and Mrs. Pinkston wouldn't press charges, as long as Drake stayed behind bars overnight and then promised not to go back to that house where you're staying."

The scout glanced sharply at the lawman. "How do you know I'm staying there?"

"Just an educated guess," Travis said lightly. "You seemed to have plenty of friends there."

"It was a good guess," White Elk said, but he did not elaborate. He did not feel like telling Travis everything that had happened since his arrival in Abilene, nor would he mention Pierre's connection with the whorehouse.

The two men strolled down the street, and after a moment Travis said, "Hogan said that renegades killed some farmer down by the border. It was probably Buffalo Knife, but there's no proof. That's the only report we've received of Indian trouble."

"Don't get your hopes up, Marshal. I know the man. He'll be here sooner or later . . . unless somebody kills him first. And I don't think there are many people in Kansas who are capable of doing it."

"Other than you, you mean."

"That's right," White Elk said. "Other than me."

* * *

Inside the jail, Sergeant Virgil Drake sat on one of the hard bunks in his cell and seethed. The corporal lay stretched out on the other bunk, snoring. In the next cell, two of the privates had claimed the bunks, while the third man lay curled on the floor wrapped in an extra blanket that Cody had tossed through the bars. All of them were asleep.

At the moment, Drake was not sure he would ever sleep again. Rage had burned the whiskey out of his system, and he was wide awake. All he could think about was the galling fact that he was sitting in a *civilian* jail. It was just about the most degrading thing that could happen to a man. And it was all that stinking redskin's fault.

Duquesne had more than Buffalo Knife and his braves to worry about now, the sergeant schemed. If the renegades did not finish off the half-breed, Virgil Drake would settle the score.

Chapter Nine

BUFFALO KNIFE STARED STONILY AT WILEY PEAKE. The Kiowa raised a hand and pointed to the north. "You are sure Abilene lies there, white man?" he asked.

Wiley nodded emphatically, and sweat beaded on his forehead. "Yep," he said. "Me and my brother cáme through there when we was first on our way to our farm. Can't be more'n twenty miles due north of here."

The white man swallowed nervously. He had been living in mortal terror ever since Buffalo Knife and the Kiowa warriors had killed his brother and kidnapped him a few days ago. The image of Calvin's bloody corpse haunted him.

In sheer terror, he had done everything Buffalo Knife asked. He had shown the Indians the best trails and steered them away from settlements. The Army had to be looking for this band of renegades, but Wiley had helped them avoid the patrols.

Now he was hoping—no, praying—that Buffalo Knife would be grateful enough to spare his life.

The Kiowa leader turned to one of his men and grated a command in his guttural tongue. Wiley licked his lips and watched intently as the brave nodded and wheeled his horse around. The Indian called to several of the others, and they rode away, yipping and howling as they headed west.

Buffalo Knife's group had grown steadily. Braves seemed to appear from nowhere to speak a few words and then join the band. Wiley knew that word of the renegades was spreading. Lone Indians on the run and smaller groups of warriors who had fled their reservations were flocking to Buffalo Knife's cause. Glancing at the braves behind him, Wiley realized that there were at least two dozen mounted Indians, not counting the ones who had just ridden off.

It was a formidable group, maybe not large enough to take the whole town of Abilene but certainly sufficient to wreak bloody havoc.

Buffalo Knife turned to Wiley and smiled. Wiley was stunned: It was the first time the farmer had seen such an expression on the savage's face.

"You have done well, white man," the chieftain said. "You were wise to tell the truth. That is the only reason you are still alive."

Wiley nervously wiped the back of his hand across his mouth. "I just tried to do right by you, Buffalo Knife. Now I reckon you'll do right by me, won't you?"

"Have you been mistreated?"

Wiley had to admit that he had not been. Except to guard him to be sure he did not run off, the Indians had left him alone. He had lived in constant fear of torture, but it had not happened.

"You have been good to me," Wiley replied.

"Are there any towns between here and the place called Abilene?"

Wiley shook his head. "Not that I know of. Ain't been through these parts in a couple of years, though, so I can't say for sure."

Solemnly, Buffalo Knife nodded. "Then we do not need your help any longer, Wiley Peake."

Wiley grinned. "Thanks, Buffalo Knife. I-I guess I better get started back to my place."

Buffalo Knife said nothing. Then, with a quick flip of his hand toward the south, he casually dismissed Wiley.

The farmer was still too terrified to feel relieved; all he wanted was to put as much distance between him and this band as possible. Hurriedly, he turned his horse and banged his heels against its flanks. It broke into a trot.

Wiley had gone less than ten feet when Buffalo Knife whipped the big blade from its sheath on his hip. Soundlessly, the knife revolved once in the air and then thumped into Wiley Peake's back. The force of the throw was such that the blade penetrated to the hilt. The point plunged into Wiley's heart, killing him instantly. He pitched off the horse's back and sprawled in the dirt.

Buffalo Knife glanced at the farmer's body only long enough to take satisfaction in the accuracy of his killing throw. Then he gestured curtly to one of the braves to retrieve his blade. He looked to the north, toward Abilene.

Everything was going according to plan. He and his men would lie low here for a few days, within striking distance of Abilene, while the warriors he had sent to the west struck a series of hit-and-run raids. Buffalo Knife knew how white men thought —the Army and the settlers would look at the raids in the western half of the state and assume that Buffalo Knife had gone there. The soldiers would hurry to the west to capture him, never realizing that he was waiting right under their noses.

Then, when the town of Abilcne believed that the danger had passed, he would strike!

He would bring fire and blood to the white men and death to the hated half-breed, White Elk Duquesne.

Luke Travis had known from the start that it would be difficult to keep secret the fact that Abilene might be attacked by Indians. Once Sergeant Drake had let it slip at Grace Pinkston's house, it became impossible.

The next morning, an angry delegation of citizens stormed into his office and demanded to know what he intended to do about the problem. Travis looked at them with a wry expression on his face and wondered how these fine upstanding citizens had learned something that had been known only to a houseful of prostitutes the night before. At least one of these men must have gone to Grace's house.

The marshal glanced at Cody, who was lounging

in the cellblock doorway, looking relieved that he did not have to deal directly with these angry citizens.

"Just take it easy, men," Travis said sharply, cutting through their babble. "I know only too well how dangerous this situation is, and I'm working with Captain Hogan to make sure the town stays safe."

"How can you guarantee that, Marshal? There's a horde of murdering savages on their way here," demanded Matthew Brown. The new apothecary slammed a fist on Travis's desk for emphasis, but the icy glare on the marshal's face made him step back involuntarily.

"Hogan's cavalry troop has been ordered to stay and guard the town until Buffalo Knife and his men have been captured," Travis said firmly. "The captain has been regularly sending out patrols to look for the Indians."

"One cavalry troop's not enough to stop an Indian raid," Thurman Simpson, the schoolteacher, protested.

"We don't know how many warriors Buffalo Knife has with him," Travis argued. "It was a pretty small band that broke off that reservation in Indian Territory."

Simpson shot back, "That's right, we don't know how many of them there are, Marshal. This renegade force may have grown ten times."

"I doubt that," Travis snapped, but he knew that the man could be right.

"That damned half-breed is causing this problem," another man cried. "If he hadn't come here, we wouldn't be in any danger."

"Duquesne's got a right to go where he pleases," said Cody. "You men have forgotten that this is the frontier. It's not going to be safe all the time. That's part of the price of settling it." The deputy's voice was angry but tightly controlled.

Travis looked at Cody in surprise. He was no longer lounging against the door, and his face was cold and grim. It was rare for the young man to speak so seriously; most of the time Cody seemed to worry about nothing more important than which pretty girl to ask to the next town dance. But Travis knew Cody liked White Elk Duquesne.

"Duquesne's not the problem," Travis said. "He's offered to leave town, but that wouldn't do any good at this point. We have no choice now; we have to wait things out. The Army is looking for Buffalo Knife all over Indian Territory and Kansas. They'll probably run him to ground long before he gets anywhere near Abilene."

"I hope so, Marshal," one of the visitors said fervently. "We all do." The others muttered their agreement, then they all turned and marched out of the office. Travis watched them go, unsure what they would do. As this news spread through town, people would either panic or stay calm. At this moment, Travis was betting on panic.

Cody stalked to the open door, glanced at the departing citizens, and then turned toward the desk with a disgusted look on his face. He shook his head and said, "Those folks have forgotten what it's like to have to settle a place. Nobody gets handed anything out here."

"Nowadays they sometimes do," Travis said. "I remember the old days, and you've heard enough about them to know how it was, Cody. But a lot of those men have never faced anything more dangerous than the general store being out of coffee. We need to remember that when they get worried about Indians." The marshal smiled. "Shoot, the thought of trading bullets with a bunch of Kiowa warriors doesn't appeal to me, either."

"I just hate to think about having to rely on those men to help defend this town," Cody said.

Travis nodded slowly.

That evening Travis was enjoying a quiet dinner with Aileen Bloom in the Sunrise Café. At the tinkling of the doorbell, the marshal looked up from his steak and potatoes and saw Captain Jonathan Hogan hurrying across the room toward him.

"I've just had a telegram from headquarters, Marshal," Hogan began excitedly. "They've heard from the officer commanding a patrol near Scott City. A band of Kiowa renegades attacked a nearby ranch and then escaped."

Travis felt his pulse quicken. "You think it was Buffalo Knife?" he asked as he set his fork down.

"That's a reasonable assumption. There hasn't been any Indian trouble in that area for quite some time, and Buffalo Knife's band has the only hostile Indians at large right now."

Travis leaned back in his chair and mulled over Hogan's news. Then he gestured to the officer to sit down and said distractedly, "Captain, I don't think you've met the town doctor. This is Aileen Bloom. Aileen, Captain Jonathan Hogan."

Hogan smiled at her and took the hand she offered him. "I'm charmed, Doctor. I must say you're a distinct improvement over our Army surgeons."

"Thank you, Captain. But I have great respect for your medical officers. They do a good job under difficult circumstances."

"Granted." Hogan turned to Travis. "What do you think, Marshal? Do you believe that Buffalo Knife has swung away from us?"

The lawman took a deep breath. He wanted to believe it. Scott City was a long way from Abilene, and if the Kiowas were that far west, it was unlikely they would cause trouble here. But instinct told Travis to be cautious.

"Why would he head west when the man he's sworn to kill is here in Abilene?" Travis asked.

"We can't be sure he knew where White Elk was," Hogan said. "We're positive he tortured that poor Crow scout he kidnapped from the reservation, but that doesn't mean the man told Buffalo Knife what he wanted to know."

Travis shook his head doubtfully. "Not many men can stand up under Indian torture, not even another Indian."

"Is Buffalo Knife familiar with this area?" Aileen asked.

"Not that we know of," Hogan answered. "He's spent most of his time in Texas and in the Indian Territory."

"Then perhaps he's simply lost," Aileen suggested.

Travis and Hogan looked at each other for a long

moment, and then the marshal nodded. Sometimes the simplest answers were the best. "That's possible," he said. "At least we can hope so."

He had been doing a lot of hoping lately. All day he had made himself visible on the streets of Abilene, answering worried questions from the townspeople and doing his best to ease their fears while still being realistic about the potential danger. So far, that approach seemed to be working. The panic he had expected had not developed. A few men had told him that they were going to pack up their families and head east until Buffalo Knife had been either killed or captured, but Travis did not expect that more than a handful of people would do that.

Now, with Hogan's news, there was a chance that everything would stay calm and quiet in Abilene. Several of the customers in the café had overheard their conversation, and Travis knew that word of the Indian attacks in the western part of the state would spread quickly.

"I'd best be getting back to camp," Hogan said as he stood up. "I just wanted to give you the news immediately."

"Thanks," Travis said. "Maybe we'll hear that Buffalo Knife's been captured in a day or two."

Hogan smiled and nodded, then said good night to Aileen. As she and Travis resumed their meal, conversation was buzzing around them. Aileen looked at Travis thoughtfully. "You don't look convinced, Luke," she said.

"I'm not," he declared flatly. "I'll believe it when Buffalo Knife is either dead or back on the reservation. Not before."

He knew he was being pessimistic, but he could not help it. All of his instincts told him that trouble was still on the horizon.

However, as the next couple of days passed and more Indian raids in the western half of the state were reported, Travis began to feel a bit optimistic. Several families did load their wagons and pull out, promising to return later. But most of Abilene's citizens went about their business as usual.

At dusk three days after Hogan had reported the Indian raid near Scott City, Travis was in Orion's Tavern. For the first time in days, he had begun to relax. He was leaning on the bar, enjoying a mug of cold beer while Orion spun a long, bawdy yarn that was punctuated by occasional squawks from Old Bailey the parrot.

White Elk Duquesne pushed open the batwings. When he saw the scout, Travis was reminded of the nerve-racking threat. The marshal suddenly tensed again, but he forced himself to grin when the scout raised a hand in greeting and moved to the bar.

"Hello, Marshal," White Elk said. "How are you, Orion?"

"I be fine, lad," Orion replied in his booming voice. "An' ye?"

"Doing all right, I suppose."

Travis had not seen White Elk since his battle with Virgil Drake, and he supposed that the scout had been staying pretty close to home. The man had to know that the townspeople would be even less fond of him now that they were aware of the threat he had inadvertently exposed them to.

White Elk turned to Travis and went on, "I've

been hearing that Buffalo Knife is a long way west of here. Is that true?"

"Appears to be," Travis said. He paused to sip his beer. "Hogan's headquarters has sent several telegrams, advising him of the raids. The renegades have hit quite a few ranches and farms. There's no doubt that they were being led by a Kiowa war chief."

White Elk nodded. "If they keep that up, the Army will catch them. It's just a matter of time."

"Do you think it's possible that Buffalo Knife's lost?"

The scout was silent for a moment as he thought over the question. Finally he said, "If it weren't for the reports that Hogan has been getting, I would doubt it. But Buffalo Knife's never been this far north and east. I suppose he could have taken a wrong turn somewhere and wound up out there, but I'd lay odds he's figured out his mistake by now. He's going to head in this direction sooner or later—if he gets the chance."

Orion laid the palms of his massive hands on the bar. "Enow o' this talk, lad. Kin I get ye a drink?"

White Elk grinned. "I'd like that, Orion. I'd like that a lot. I think I'll just have a beer, like the marshal here."

Ignoring the dismayed looks that some of the customers were casting his way, Orion picked up a mug and drew the beer. Travis saw the looks and knew that White Elk did, too, but all three men paid no attention to them. The scout was not well-liked in Abilene, but Travis and Orion had never let public opinion stop them from doing what they believed was right.

White Elk picked up the mug that Orion slid across the bar and took an appreciative sip. He was just licking the foam from his lips when the batwings swung open and Captain Hogan strode into the tavern, followed by Cody Fisher.

Hogan came directly to the bar, gave White Elk a curt nod, and then said to Travis, "Good evening, Marshal. I wanted to let you know that I've just received another telegram from headquarters."

"News of another raid out west?" Travis asked.

Hogan shook his head. "New orders," he said.

Travis noticed the captain's grim expression, and he swiftly leaped to the logical conclusion. "You've been ordered to pull out of Abilene," the marshal said shrewdly.

Hogan shook his head. "Not quite, but you've made a good assumption," he said. "I've been instructed to split my forces and send half of my troop to Hays City, where they will join the hunt for Buffalo Knife. I'll have to put one of my corporals in command until they reach Hays."

"Why don't you send Drake?" White Elk asked.

"I prefer to keep Sergeant Drake with me," Hogan replied shortly. "He's an experienced soldier, and I rely on him a great deal."

The marshal sensed the real reason behind Hogan's brusque words. The captain wanted to keep Drake where he could ride herd on him. The sergeant obviously had a penchant for getting into trouble.

The marshal said nothing about his conclusions. Instead, he commented, "I don't much like the idea of splitting your force in two. We still can't be certain that Buffalo Knife won't show up here."

"That's true. But the officers at headquarters evidently feel differently, and I have to follow my orders, Marshal."

"Of course," Travis said.

"My men will be pulling out in the morning," Hogan went on. "I'll continue to send patrols out to watch for trouble, but it's going to be more difficult now. We're going to be spread pretty thin."

"We'll do what we can."

Hogan nodded. He said good night and walked out of the tavern. No one was surprised that he had not stopped for a drink.

"Well, we didn't need the cavalry in the first place," Cody said with a cocky grin on his face. "Orion, how about drawing me one of those brews?"

"Aye," the Scotsman rumbled. "But I'm not so sure 'bout those soldier boys. They could come in handy."

Cody kept grinning, but he nodded slowly as he considered Orion's words. "You might be right at that," he finally said.

Chapter Ten

WHITE ELK DID NOT STAY IN ORION'S TAVERN FOR very long. The resentful glances from the other customers made him too uncomfortable. He finished his beer, said good night to Travis, Cody, and Orion, then went outside to mount his horse. He turned the sorrel toward Grace Pinkston's.

It was not much better on the street. Quite a few people were still on the boardwalks, and as he rode down Texas Street, he saw them staring coldly at him. He forced himself to look straight ahead into the gathering twilight.

A large part of him wanted to just keep riding, to put Abilene behind him and leave it there. It was beginning to look as if the danger from Buffalo Knife was not going to materialize. The Army would soon run the renegades to ground, White Elk told himself. He would not be putting anyone in jeopardy if he left.

Besides, this visit had not worked out the way he had hoped it would. There had been no real reconciliation with his father; the friction between him and Pierre was still as strong as ever.

As for Rita Nivens . . . He was genuinely fond of her, and they had a wonderful time together in bed, but neither one had ever seen their relationship as permanent. Grace and Malachi had become his friends, but that bond was not strong enough to hold him.

As he reached the intersection of Walnut and Third streets, he looked toward the other end of town where his father and Lora lived. He had to admit it—Lora was the only reason he was unwilling to leave Abilene.

From what Aileen Bloom had said, the impending birth might be very dangerous for Lora. Knowing the way his father felt, White Elk could not just ride out of town now. Lora would be giving birth any day.

Besides, he wanted to see his new half brother or sister before he left.

He rode slowly to Grace's, certain that staying in Abilene was the right thing to do.

The next morning White Elk slept late. By the time he awoke, it was nearly noon. He stretched, relishing the feel of his skin against the sheets, enjoying the warmth of Rita snuggled against him.

She stirred, moving closer. He leaned over her

and gently kissed her. Rita purred contentedly and slid her hands down his body.

"I can't stay right now," he said softly.

She lazily opened her green eyes and looked up at him. "Why not? There's no place you have to be, is there?"

"I'm afraid there is."

Rita stiffened in his arms, then abruptly rolled away from him. She turned onto her side and faced the wall. "I know where you're going," she said coldly. "The same place you go every day. To see her."

White Elk could not deny that he had been spending more time at his father's house the last few days. Lora seemed to enjoy his visits, and he could keep an eye on her and make sure she was not pushing herself too hard. Pierre had made several freight runs in recent days, too, and Lora would have been left alone had White Elk not gone to check on her. He had wondered if Pierre was trying to avoid him. If so, White Elk did not really care. He was much more interested in Lora now.

"That's where you're going, isn't it?" Rita prodded.

He nodded. "I'm not used to seeing jealousy from you, Rita. It's not like you."

"You've known me for only a few days," she replied without looking at him. "What do you really know about me, except that I'm a whore?"

White Elk touched her shoulder and stroked her soft skin. "I know that you're very special," he said quietly. "You've treated me well. You've been a friend."

"I've been more than that," Rita shot back. "And you know it."

He sighed. "Yes, I suppose you have. But you've always known that I'd be riding on sooner or later. I've already been in Abilene a lot longer than I intended to be."

"The only reason you're staying is because of her."

He could not argue with that, but she made it sound all wrong. "She's my stepmother," he said.

Rita rolled over, her eyes flashing. "Is that all she is to you?" she demanded.

"My God, Rita," he exclaimed. "The woman's about to have a baby!"

Rita shook her head. "That doesn't mean anything. I've heard men say that women are never prettier than when they're in the family way. Is that what you think, White Elk?"

He did not reply. Instead, he swung his legs out of bed and stood up. Clearly, her resentment of Lora had been building for quite a while.

"You're wrong, Rita," he finally said, as he pulled on his clothes. "There's nothing between Lora and me but affection. I'm sorry if that disturbs you."

Rita threw back the sheet and stood up. She stalked to the dressing table to pick up the robe she had flung there the night before. As he watched the smooth movement of her sleek nude body, he thought fleetingly that he was crazy. Any normal man would not walk out now: He would grab her and toss her onto that bed and spend the afternoon loving her. . . .

He walked to the door with his hat in his hand

and said, "I'll be back later." Then he stepped out of the room and quietly closed the door behind him.

Pausing for a moment in the hall, White Elk took a deep breath. Fool or not, he knew what he had to do. Lora had been complaining of some new pains yesterday, and he wanted to be sure she was all right.

He was grateful that he did not see Grace or Malachi as he left the house. They would see the look on his face and know that something was wrong, and he was in no mood to explain anything.

Besides, he thought with a grim little smile as he got his horse from the stable, he was not sure that he could explain things. Many of the emotions he had been feeling lately made no sense to him.

Perhaps deep inside he felt something more for Lora than simple affection. As unlikely as it seemed, maybe he did have some romantic interest in his stepmother. All he knew for sure was that she was sweet and kind and seemed to light up when she saw his face.

He shook his head as he swung the sorrel down the street. Lora was Pierre's wife, was about to become the mother of his child.

White Elk tied his horse in front of Pierre's house and strolled up the walk to the porch. He rapped lightly on the door and waited. When there was no response after a moment, he knocked again, a little harder this time. Still no one came to the door.

With a worried frown creasing his forehead, he pulled the screen door open and tried the knob of the inner door. It turned easily, which was no surprise; it was rare for anyone to lock a door around here. He pushed it open and stepped tentatively inside.

"Pa?" he called. "Lora? Anybody home?"

A footstep at the far end of the hallway told him that he was not alone after all. Lora appeared in the kitchen doorway, her features tight with strain, her skin pale. When she saw him, though, she gave a wan smile.

"Hello, White Elk," she said. "I'm sorry I couldn't get to the door. I'm moving a little slowly today."

Without thinking, White Elk hurried to her, put his arm around her shoulders, and let her lean on him. "What's wrong, Lora?" he asked anxiously.

She shook her head. "Nothing's wrong, White Elk. I'm just tired and a bit uncomfortable. Everything is fine."

"You're not . . ."

She shook her head, her smile a little more easy now as she heard the embarrassment in his voice. "Don't worry," she told him. "It's not time yet. At least I don't think it is."

As he helped her into the parlor, he thought she sounded uncertain. Lora sank into one of the chairs with a grateful sigh.

"I'll be fine now," she said. "I am glad you came by. I was beginning to worry a little."

"Where's Pierre?" White Elk asked, trying to keep the anger out of his voice. His father had no right to leave Lora alone at a time like this.

"He went to Junction City with a freight wagon early this morning. He said he would be back tonight."

White Elk took a deep breath and stalked to the window. Staring out at the bright sunlit street, he tried valiantly to control his temper before turning to face her. "What was he thinking about?" he asked at last. "You should have someone with you all the time now."

Lora's expression grew stern. "I told him to go, White Elk," she said in her husband's defense. "I told him I would be just fine by myself for the day."

"That's what he wants to think," the scout blurted. "I've talked to Dr. Bloom, Lora. There's a good chance you're going to have trouble with this birth!"

As soon as the words were out of his mouth, White Elk wished desperately that he could reclaim them. He saw the the sudden flash of fear in Lora's eyes. She might have sensed that she was in danger, but now, in his anger at Pierre, White Elk had confirmed it. Mentally cursing his father, he hurried over and knelt beside her chair.

"I didn't mean that the way it sounded," he began, but Lora cut him off.

"It's all right, White Elk," she said softly. She was already recovering her composure. "I understand how worried you are. After all, this is your brother or sister we're talking about."

"And my stepmother," he said.

Lora waved a hand. "I told you, don't worry about me. All I'll be doing is what women have been doing for centuries. It's nothing special."

White Elk suddenly knew that was not true: It was very special.

Lora put her hands on the arms of the chair and

began to push herself up. "Look, I'm feeling better now. Why don't I fix us some lunch?"

Looking closely at her, White Elk saw that her color did seem a little better, but he placed his hands on her shoulders and gently eased her back. "I don't think so. You sit there and rest. I'll fix the meal." He grinned. "You'll find that I can fix a few things besides beans and flapjacks and hardtack."

Lora returned the smile. "All right. There's a ham in the smokehouse."

White Elk nodded. "I'll see to it."

He spent the next half hour preparing their lunch. Over his objections, Lora moved into the kitchen and talked with him as he worked.

"I don't want you to think that I'm unhappy here White Elk, but my baby is going to have an even better place to live than Abilene. Pierre has promised that someday we'll move East. I want my baby to have a good education and all the advantages that a big city can offer."

"Just because a place is big doesn't mean it's the best place to be," White Elk replied. "Me, I'd never be happy cooped up in some place where I couldn't see the sun or smell the earth or feel the breeze on my face."

"But you were raised in the outdoors. That's the only kind of life you know. Surely you can see how it would be better to live in civilization."

He did not want to argue with her, so he grunted noncommittally and went on with his work. Maybe she was right, but as far as he was concerned, civilization was overrated. From what he had heard, it was easier to get killed in the back alleys of some big city than it was in the open spaces of the frontier. At least out here a man had a better than even chance to survive, provided he was strong, resourceful, and above all stubborn.

If he ever had a child, he thought, he would want the youngster to know the lonely places, to see the splendor of a grassy valley, to experience the spectacular displays of a mountain thunderstorm, to feel the sun and the wind, and to know what it meant to be truly alive. Those things were just as important as anything so-called civilization could offer.

He doubted that he would ever have a child. He did not live the kind of life that would attract a woman, not the marrying kind of woman. There were always painted ladies like Rita Nevins to take care of his physical needs.

After they had eaten, Lora complimented him on his cooking. White Elk grinned and said, "If a man doesn't want to put up with Army food, he's got to learn to fend for himself. A matter of survival, I guess you could say."

"You're not fond of the Army, are you?" she asked.

"Not very. I never cared for all the rules and regulations. But they're doing a job that has to be done, and my work isn't too bad when I'm out scouting and don't have some eager young officer looking over my shoulder all the time."

Talking about the Army made him think about Buffalo Knife. He had not told Lora about the renegade, and he decided not to tell her now. She seemed to feel better, and he did not want to upset her with tales about some murdering savage. But the danger from Buffalo Knife was just one reason why he was having doubts about going back to the Army. He was going to have to think about finding some other way of putting his talents to work for him.

He steered the conversation away from the Army while he cleaned the dishes and then helped Lora to the parlor. When she was settled in her chair, she said, "Would you mind going into my sewing room and getting the project I'm working on, White Elk?"

"Not at all," he replied. "What is it?"

She smiled. "I'm knitting something. You'll know it when you see it."

With a puzzled shrug, he turned and went into the hall. During an earlier visit she had shown him the sewing room on the other side of the hall, toward the rear of the house. He went in and saw the spool of white yarn, the knitting needles, and a partially completed garment lying on a table. He picked them up and started back to the parlor.

As he went, he unfolded the garment and saw that it was a tiny sweater. A tender feeling swelled inside him. To think that anything small enough to wear this could be alive, a special little being who under Lora's guidance would grow into a fine adult.

Grinning sheepishly, he went into the parlor and handed her the knitting. "Looks like fine work," he said.

"It's done with love," she replied simply. "That makes it special."

The two of them spent the afternoon quietly and

pleasantly sitting in the parlor, sometimes talking, sometimes just enjoying companionable silences. White Elk had not planned to spend the entire afternoon here, but with Pierre gone and Lora shakier than usual, he could not leave her alone. She had had no more pains since his arrival, but with the baby due at any time, he thought it would be wise for him to stay.

He knew that Rita was probably seething because he had not returned, but he could do nothing about that. As pleasant as his stay at Grace's had been, if it was coming to an end that was all right with him. Nothing lasted forever.

As the deep shadows of dusk began to darken the parlor, he went to the kitchen to prepare a light meal from the luncheon leftovers. He helped Lora from her chair in the parlor and gave her his arm to escort her to the dining room.

As she settled at the table, she said, "Pierre should be back soon. Won't he be surprised to see how helpful you've been? I really appreciate everything you've done, White Elk."

"It was no bother," he said gruffly. He was still uncomfortable with her praise and gratitude; he was not used to such treatment. And he would never expect his father to express such sentiments.

Lora picked up her fork and leaned toward her plate; then she suddenly dropped the utensil. It clattered to the floor. She clutched at her swollen belly as she uttered a surprised, breathless "Oh!"

Instantly, White Elk was beside her. "What is it?" he asked anxiously.

"A pain . . ." Lora replied weakly. "I . . . I

didn't expect it to hurt so bad . . . but I'm sure I'll be all ri—"

She broke off as another gasp escaped from her lips. Her face, already pale, grew more ashen.

"Oh, my God," White Elk breathed. "It's time, isn't it? It's the baby."

Lora looked up at him and forced herself to smile. "I—I'm afraid it is," she said. "I'm sorry you had to be here to . . . to see me like this."

White Elk pushed away his own worries. Panicking now would be the worst thing he could do for Lora. Dr. Bloom had told him to fetch her as soon as Lora started having labor pains, so that was what he would do.

The front door opened at that moment, and booted feet clumped into the hall. "I'm back, Lora," Pierre Duquesne called. "Where are you?"

"We're in the dining room," White Elk rapped. "You'd better get in here, Pa!"

A moment later Pierre appeared in the doorway, frowning darkly as he peered across the table at them. White Elk was hovering worriedly over Lora with his arm around her shoulders for support.

"Well, this is a fine sight to greet a man when he comes home tired from working," Pierre growled. "The way you're pawin' my woman, boy, if I didn't know better I'd say *you* planted the seed for that whelp, 'stead of me."

White Elk stared at his father. Pierre was swaying slightly, and his eyes were red-rimmed and glazed. White Elk thought disgustedly, *The man is about to become a father, and he's drunk!*

"Lora needs help," White Elk said tightly. "It's

her time. I have to get the doctor; you need to stay
with her."

Pierre reached into the pocket of his coat and
took out a flask. "I'll stay," he said as he uncapped
it. "And you can damn well go, but I don't want
you bringin' no sawbones back here. Don't need
'em." He tipped the flask to his mouth and took a
long swallow.

White Elk could stand no more of his father's
drunken arrogance. Ignoring Lora's warning hand
on his arm, he blazed, "You booze-soaked old
bastard! Can't you see your wife is about to have a
baby? She needs help!"

Pierre leveled a finger at him. "Shut your mouth,
boy!" he bellowed. "You're in my house, and you'll
show some respect, dammit! Now get your hands
off my wife and get out of here!"

Lora cried in pain once more. White Elk glanced
down at her. The spasms were gripping her regularly now, a sure sign that the child was on the way.
And he could tell from the look on her face that the
pains were intense.

"What about the doctor?" he asked Pierre.

"There was no doctor anywhere around when
your ma had you, and she did just fine," Pierre
insisted. "Bad enough Lora wants to be pampered
by havin' some pill-pusher here, but I'll be damned
if I'll ever let a woman doctor set foot in this
house!"

"That's your final word on it?" White Elk rasped.

Pierre's answer was to take another swig from his
flask.

White Elk's hand tightened on Lora's shoulder.

He looked down at her and said, "Don't worry, I'll bring Aileen Bloom. Let me help you to your bed before I go."

"I . . . I think that would be a good idea," Lora said.

Pierre drained the last of the whiskey and tossed the flask aside, then started angrily around the table. "I told you to get away from my wife!" he snapped. He balled his fists and swung.

White Elk saw the fist hurtling toward his head and let his instincts take over. He darted smoothly to the side, and Pierre's punch flailed at empty air. White Elk stepped forward and hooked his right hand into Pierre's belly.

The older man gasped, doubled over, and staggered back. White Elk might have followed with another punch if Lora had not clutched at his arm and cried, "White Elk, no! Please, leave him alone!"

The scout glanced down at his stepmother. "You really do love him, don't you?"

"Of course I do. He's my husband." Despite what she was going through, Lora's voice was strong.

White Elk nodded abruptly. Ignoring Pierre, he helped Lora to her feet and walked with her toward the hall. "We don't have any time to waste," he told her. "I'll get you into the bedroom, and then I'll go for Dr. Bloom."

Her fingers tightened on his arm. "Please hurry," she whispered.

White Elk heard Pierre floundering around behind them. He glanced quickly over his shoulder and saw his father was holding his stomach with one hand. Pierre was holding himself up with the other hand flat on the table.

Within a matter of moments, White Elk had Lora lying on the bed in her room. Her forehead was glistening with sweat, and she chewed her lower lip to keep from crying out as the pains racked her. White Elk smoothed a stray lock of blond hair from her forehead and tried to smile reassuringly.

"I'll be right back," he promised her. "You just hold on."

"I . . . I'll be here," she replied, gamely returning his smile.

He patted her shoulder, then hurried from the room and ran to the front door. As he rushed past the parlor, he saw that Pierre was now slumped in one of the chairs. He was staring at the rug on the floor and holding another bottle in his hand.

No, the scout thought grimly as he vaulted the picket fence to his horse, *Pierre Duquesne has not changed at all.*

White Elk banged his heels against the sorrel's flanks and urged the animal to a gallop. Aileen Bloom's office was only minutes away, but the ride seemed an eternity to him. He could imagine Lora's agony back at his father's house.

When he finally reined his horse to a stop in front of the office, he saw that luck was with him. The doctor and Luke Travis were just stepping through the front door onto the porch. Aileen was carrying her black medical bag.

As White Elk dropped from the saddle and ran

toward them, Travis rushed down the walk. "What's wrong, White Elk?" he asked, grabbing the frantic scout's arm.

"It's Lora!" he gasped. Looking past Travis at Aileen, he cried, "It's her time, Doctor. You've got to come quick."

"Of course," Aileen said briskly. "I'll just get my carriage—"

"There's no time for that!" White Elk exclaimed. "She's in so much pain."

"All right." Aileen turned to Travis. "Luke, would you mind giving me a ride?"

Travis grinned and reached out to take the bag from her hand. "Come on," he said as he hurried toward his horse, which was tied up in front of the office.

As White Elk mounted up again, the marshal got on first, then held his hand out to Aileen. She grasped it and swung up behind him.

"Hold on," Travis grunted. He wheeled his horse and urged it to a gallop behind White Elk's mount.

Time still seemed to drag for the scout, but at last they reached Pierre Duquesne's house. White Elk sprang from his mount and ran up the walk, anxious to see if Lora was all right. Travis helped Aileen down, and they quickly followed him.

As White Elk stepped onto the porch, the front door flew open. Pierre, swaying wildly, loomed in the doorway. In the time he had been gone, White Elk thought, Pierre had probably finished that bottle.

Pierre stared blearily past White Elk and glared at Travis and Aileen, who were about to climb onto the porch. He grabbed his son's arm and growled,

"I told you not to bring that damned sawbones back here!"

"Get out of my way, old man!" White Elk shoved Pierre aside.

Pierre staggered back a step, then reached into his coat. He whipped out a pistol and leveled it at White Elk. "Hold it right there!" he ordered harshly. "I'm tired of you tryin' to boss me around, boy. This is my house, and my word is law, you hear!"

White Elk, Travis, and Aileen froze. The scout stared at his father in disbelief. After a moment of tense silence Travis said, "No, Duquesne, I represent the law around here, and I'm telling you to put that gun down."

Pierre looked belligerently at the marshal. "Doesn't a man have the right to protect his own wife?" he demanded. "Haven't seen a doctor yet who didn't do more harm than good!"

"You're not trying to protect anyone," White Elk said. A muffled cry came from inside the house, and he knew that it came from Lora. It took all of his willpower to keep from leaping at his father, gun or no gun. "You're just trying to impose your will on everyone, like the arrogant fool you are."

"Your wife needs help, Mr. Duquesne," Aileen said in a calm voice. "I'm sure once you think about it, you'll see that we're just trying to help her."

Pierre drunkenly swung the gun's muzzle back and forth between White Elk and Travis. "You go to hell, lady!"

"That's enough, Duquesne," Travis snapped angrily. "Put the gun down. We're going in, and if you try to stop us, I'll do whatever I have to."

The gun wavered slightly. Pierre had lived in Abilene long enough to know about Luke Travis's reputation with a gun. White Elk held his breath. He wanted to help Lora more than anything, but he did not want to see his father gunned down.

Pierre let the pistol droop. With a grimace, he stepped aside.

White Elk heaved a sigh of relief as he ducked through the door. Aileen swept in behind him. Travis stepped onto the porch and started past Pierre. Suddenly, Pierre's face contorted with rage, and he lifted the gun to slash at Travis's head.

The marshal flung his left arm up to block the blow as his right fist smashed into Pierre's jaw. Pierre flew back and slammed against the wall of the house. The marshal's hand closed over the cylinder of Pierre's pistol and wrenched the weapon free. As he stepped back quickly, he whipped his Colt from its holster.

"You'd best stay right where you are, Duquesne," Travis grated. "I'd almost enjoy putting a bullet in you right now."

Inside the house, White Elk and Aileen had reached Lora's bedroom. As she questioned Lora in a soothing voice, Aileen checked her pulse. Lora gasped out the answers between her cries of pain.

"The contractions are very close together now," Aileen said to White Elk, who was hovering anxiously near the bedside. "I'll need clean sheets and some hot water to sterilize my instruments. Can you tend to that?"

The scout nodded. "Right away," he said. He was

glad to have something to do; the tasks would distract him.

White Elk walked quickly to the kitchen. He started a fire in the stove, set a pot of water on to boil, then went to look for clean linen. By the time he found some in a hall closet and hurried back to Lora's room with it, Aileen had finished her preliminary examination.

The look on the doctor's face sent a shudder of panic up White Elk's spine. "What is it?" he asked.

Aileen shook her head, leaned over Lora, and wiped the beads of sweat that glistened on her forehead. "You rest for a moment, Lora," Aileen said quietly. "I'll be right back."

Placing a hand on White Elk's arm, Aileen drew him out into the hall. Clearly, she wanted to tell him something that she wanted to keep from Lora. That only increased White Elk's anxiety. He would rather face another battle, outnumbered, against hostile Quanah Parker, than live through these moments worrying about Lora.

"What's wrong?" he demanded in a low voice.

"That baby is ready to come," Aileen whispered, "but it's in the wrong position. It's what we call a breech birth. The fact that Lora's body is rather small doesn't help matters, either."

White Elk took a deep breath. "So what are we going to do?"

"I have to turn the baby so that it can emerge properly. But to do that, I'll have to wait until it's descended further so that I can reach it better. If I wait too long, it'll be too late to turn it correctly. This is a very delicate situation, White Elk."

"You can do it, can't you?"

Aileen looked at him intently, then said, "I'll do the very best I can. That's all I can do."

White Elk closed his eyes. Finally, he nodded and opened them again. "I'll do whatever I can to help," he said.

Aileen squeezed his arm. "I know you will."

Together, they returned to the room where Lora waited.

It was the longest night of White Elk's life. There was a clock on the wall opposite Lora's bed, but every time he glanced at it, the hands seemed frozen.

Long before ten, Lora was raving and thrashing from the pain. Aileen helped her through the contractions and encouraged her to rest between them, but the agony was too much for the young woman. Finally, the doctor took a needle and an ampule from her bag.

"I have to give her something to ease the pain," Aileen explained as she prepared the injection. "She'll need all her strength for the delivery. I hope this will help her through it without knocking her out."

"I thought the baby would be here by now, the way you were talking earlier," White Elk said.

"So did I," Aileen replied grimly. "Lora is in hard labor, but she isn't dilating. Until she does, I can't turn the baby."

White Elk paced over to the window and pushed back the curtain to stare into the night. He was used to facing problems that could be solved with guns and knives and fists. He had never felt so helpless in his life as he did now.

Lora cried out again, and the sound struck at his soul.

Sometime around midnight, Luke Travis appeared in the doorway and motioned for White Elk to join him. In a low voice, the marshal said, "Your pa's asleep now, White Elk. He finished off another bottle of whiskey before he passed out. He'll have quite a head in the morning."

"Just as long as he doesn't cause any more trouble tonight," White Elk replied. "Thank you for keeping an eye on him, Marshal. For a while there, I was afraid one of us was going to have to shoot him."

"So was I," Travis agreed. "Anything I can do to help in there?"

White Elk shook his head. "Not unless you'd like to say a few prayers."

Travis grinned tiredly. "Couldn't hurt," he said.

White Elk clapped a hand on the lawman's shoulder and shook his head wearily. Then he turned to enter the room again.

In the early hours of the morning, White Elk found himself leaning over Lora's bed, holding her hand tightly and uttering words of encouragement. At the foot of the bed, Aileen Bloom called excitedly, "I've got him! The baby's turned now! Bear down, Lora, push! Now!"

Sweat covered the faces of the three people. Lora shrieked in pain and effort, her back arching off the bed. Then suddenly she relaxed and went limp.

A moment later, there was a tiny, high-pitched cry.

"It's a girl!" Aileen announced in a voice that trembled with strain and relief. She worked quickly as she cleaned the baby's nose and mouth, then cut the cord.

White Elk squeezed Lora's hand, and she opened her eyes to gaze up at him. The medication Aileen had given her was starting to wear off, and White Elk could see the comprehension in his stepmother's eyes as she said, "I . . . I . . . we did it, didn't we? The baby's all right?"

White Elk glanced at Aileen and got a quick, confirming nod. "The baby's fine," he said. "It's a little girl, a beautiful little girl."

Aileen wrapped the baby in a clean sheet and moved around the bed with the precious bundle. As she placed it in Lora's arms, she said gently, "Here's your daughter."

Lora moved back the corner of the sheet and smiled at the red, wrinkled face. The baby's eyes were closed, and it was whimpering.

"She is beautiful," Lora whispered. "Don't you think so, White Elk?"

He reached out, brushed the soft skin of his half sister's cheek with a fingertip. "Lovely," he said.

He straightened, and the weariness he had held off all night suddenly flooded through him. Leaving Lora cooing and talking to the baby, he went into the hall and tried to stretch the kinks out of his muscles.

Travis, rubbing his face and neck, came out of the parlor. "Dozed off in one of the chairs," he explained with a grin. "How's the mother and baby?"

White Elk nodded at the fretful cries coming from Lora's room. "They're both doing fine. Dr. Bloom worked a miracle or two, I'd say."

"Nothing unusual for Aileen," Travis said. "Sorry your pa had to miss it."

White Elk's expression hardened. "It's his own fault. I'm not sure he deserves that lovely family he's got."

Travis shrugged. "None of my business. But I did want to stay around to make sure he didn't cause any more trouble. Also, I want to see that Aileen gets back to her place all right. We can get Mrs. Dawson to come stay with Lora. She helps with most of the new babies in town."

"Sounds fine," White Elk nodded.

Wiping her hands on a cloth, Aileen stepped into the hallway. "Well, that wasn't the most difficult birth I've witnessed, but it was bad enough," she said with a tired smile. "Luckily, everything went well. That's quite a sister you've got, White Elk."

He had to grin. "I know."

Travis said, "I told White Elk we'd see Mrs. Dawson and send her over."

"That's a good idea," Aileen said. "Can you keep an eye on things here for a little while, White Elk?"

"Of course. Thank you, Doctor, for everything you did."

"I'm just glad Lora has such a good friend as you. She wouldn't have made it otherwise."

Aileen gathered her instruments, and promising to send Mrs. Dawson over immediately, she left with Travis. White Elk walked wearily back to Lora's room and stood in the doorway watching quietly. Lora was propped up against the pillows now, cradling the baby against her. She looked over the child's downy head and met White Elk's gaze. "Thank you," she said softly. "Thank you for me . . . and for Josette."

White Elk smiled and said gently, "You're both welcome."

Chapter Eleven

—◆—

As White Elk moved to the bedside and gazed at mother and child lying in the golden ring of lamp-light, tears began to well in his eyes. Lora had named the baby after his grandmother Josette, and that touch overwhelmed him. He closed his eyes, then blinked back the tears and watched the pair with awe. Despite her pallor, Lora looked more beautiful than ever, and little Josette was a precious bundle, lovingly held in her mother's arms.

He was as tired as he had ever been in his life, but the joy that coursed through him was incredibly restoring. "You have a lot to be proud of, Lora," he said tenderly. "You have a wonderful baby, and you did a fine job."

Lora smiled at him. "I couldn't have done it

without you and Dr. Bloom." She looked past him toward the doorway. "Where's Pierre? Why hasn't he come in to see the baby? I can understand why he didn't want to be here while . . . while Josette was being born, but I thought he'd want to see her. . . ."

White Elk hesitated, unsure how much more Lora could endure tonight. He decided she would not want him to lie to her. "He's passed out from too much whiskey," he said bluntly. "I don't expect you'll see him until sometime tomorrow."

"Oh," Lora said hollowly, the joy fading from her eyes. Then she forced a smile and went on, "I suppose a man has a right to take a drink when he becomes a father."

White Elk caught his breath and controlled the anger that threatened to burst from him. If he told Lora about Pierre pulling a gun on them when he and Aileen and Travis had tried to come into the house, she would still make excuses for him. She loved him. She might not be blind to his faults, but she would not condemn him for them.

With a deep sigh he pulled a chair close to the bed and sat down. While they waited for Mrs. Dawson he and Lora spoke quietly so they would not wake the infant. Nevertheless, little Josette roused from her sleep and let out a tiny squall. Her small, fragile hand reached out blindly, and White Elk slipped his finger into it. Instinctively, Josette's fingers closed tightly on his.

"Quite a grip for a new baby," he said with a grin.

"Of course. She's going to be a strong little girl."

A knock sounded on the front door. White Elk

looked at Lora. "That must be the woman Marshal Travis said he would send over. I'll go see." Gently, he disengaged his finger from Josette's grip and stood up.

At the door was a heavyset woman with brown hair that was pulled back severely in a bun. But her open, friendly smile softened the stern impression she gave. "Hello. I'm Alice Dawson," she said warmly. "Marshal Travis and Dr. Bloom stopped at my place and said you needed some help with a new baby."

"That's right," White Elk said, returning her smile. "I'm White Elk Duquesne. Come in, I'll take you to Lora and the baby. She's my new sister, you know; her name is Josette."

"Yes, I know about you, Mr. Duquesne." He heard a disapproving note in her voice. "I'm acquainted with your father, too."

White Elk glanced over his shoulder. "Sounds like you don't care for either one of us."

"I didn't mean it that way," she said, instantly beginning to apologize. "I'm just a little worried about that Indian business everyone in town is talking about."

"I can understand that," White Elk replied evenly, soothingly. He did not want Alice Dawson to feel uncomfortable.

"And as far as your father goes, Mr. Duquesne, all I can say is that I know your stepmother fairly well. I like Lora, and I wouldn't want to see her or her baby mistreated."

"Neither would I," he said sincerely.

"Well, then, you and I will get along fine, won't we?"

White Elk grinned at her again and opened the door of Lora's room.

If he had had any doubts about Mrs. Dawson's ability to care for Lora and Josette, they vanished quickly. The older woman, who explained that she had eight children of her own, immediately took charge and shooed White Elk out of the room.

Grinning and shaking his head at his banishment, he moved down the hall and looked into the parlor to see if his father had passed out there. The parlor was empty, and White Elk began searching the other rooms. He found Pierre at last in the sewing room, sprawled on the divan. An empty whiskey bottle lay on the floor next to his dangling hand.

White Elk stood listening to his father's heavy breathing for a long moment. That whiskey-soaked brain had no idea that a little girl had been born, that a new life had begun. And Pierre would not know it until morning, if he was coherent even then.

A man could not be forced to care about his family, White Elk thought. Pierre Duquesne was living proof of that.

White Elk went to the parlor and sank gratefully into one of the chairs. It was the first time he had sat down in hours. Wearily he leaned his head against the back of the chair and let his eyes close slowly. I'll just rest for a moment, he thought—

Alice Dawson nudging his shoulder startled him out of a deep sleep.

"You'd best wake up, Mr. Duquesne," she said in a low voice. "You'll get quite a crick sleeping in a chair like that."

White Elk sat up and rubbed his already sore neck. "You're right," he said. "I'd better find a place to stretch out."

"There's no need for you to stay here," Mrs. Dawson said. "Everything is under control. The baby nursed just fine, and she and Lora are both asleep now. Dr. Bloom told me she'd come by first thing in the morning, so you feel free to go whenever you'd like."

White Elk nodded. "Thanks." He stood up, wondering what he should do next. He could sleep here on the sofa, but he imagined that Rita and Grace had to be wondering where he was by now. They might even be worrying about him. "You're sure everything's fine?" he asked Mrs. Dawson.

"Everything," she assured him.

He stepped into the foyer. His hat was on the table, placed there when he had first arrived—a lifetime ago, it seemed—and he picked it up. "In that case, I'll go on. If Lora wakes up, tell her that I'll be back tomorrow morning. This morning, really, since it's only a few hours off."

"Sure, I'd be glad to. Good night, Mr. Duquesne."

He smiled. "Good night, Mrs. Dawson."

This time as he left Pierre's house he rode at a much slower pace. The night was cool and quiet; the houses he passed, dark and peaceful. A gentle breeze blew from the west. A feeling of deep contentment swept over him, as though for the first time in a long while he could see his life clearly.

He knew he could not remain in Abilene indefinitely, just drifting along and waiting for something to happen. He would stay to help until Lora was on her feet again, but afterward it would be time to leave . . . for several reasons.

He was tired of the friction between his father and him. If there had ever been any love between them, it was gone now; Pierre had taken care of that. What he felt for Rita Nevins was not love either, and he was becoming increasingly uncomfortable staying at his father's bordello. He would have to end that even before he left Abilene. After he had gotten some sleep, he would say his goodbyes to Rita, Grace, and Malachi and start looking for a new place to stay.

But tonight he had been confronted with the most important reason he had to leave—the overwhelming tenderness that had rushed through him as he looked down at his stepmother and new half sister. He knew that he was in love with Lora Duquesne.

He now understood that he had probably felt that way from the first moment he saw her. He shook his head at the disturbing realization. Lora had treated him as a friend as well as a stepmother, but he knew that he wanted more than that from her. If he stayed, sooner or later she would find out how strongly he was attracted to her, and then she would have to choose between his father and him.

White Elk did not want that to happen. Lora loved his father. He had no right to come between them. . . .

Deep in thought, he rode on, his horse plodding slowly down Third Street.

Sergeant Virgil Drake and four cavalry troopers had been drinking in a narrow, windowless saloon called the Gem—an improbable name for a place so seedy—since early evening. Grace Pinkston's brothel might be off-limits, but Abilene's streets were lined with saloons that would welcome the soldiers.

This was the first evening Drake had had off since the brawl at Grace's, and a part of him wanted to cut loose and really howl. But he had decided to control that urge. He drank heavily, but he did not get drunk. He watched, a cold calm in his pale eyes, as his companions guzzled whiskey and took turns pawing the two tired whores who worked in the Gem as bar-girls. The troopers could have their fun. Drake knew he would take his pleasure later.

His dislike of White Elk Duquesne had grown into hate, and he had nurtured the hatred for days. Drake would have almost welcomed an attack by Buffalo Knife and his renegades; shooting a few Indians for practice would have felt good. But as time passed and nothing happened, Drake had begun to worry that he would not see any action. He had watched that morning as half the troop pulled out to head west and join in the search for Buffalo Knife. He should have been in command of that detail, he thought bitterly.

But that prig Hogan would not give it to him. As the days went by with no sign of Buffalo Knife, Virgil Drake knew that the rest of the troop would soon be withdrawn from Abilene. If that happened, Drake would have to wait to settle his score with Duquesne, and he knew he might never have another opportunity.

That was why he had to take care of things tonight. Drake had sulked and moaned and hinted until Hogan had given him the evening off just to shut him up, despite the short-handedness that the captain had complained about. Years of manipulating young shavetails had taught the wily veteran sergeant how to get what he wanted.

Drake also knew how to deal with the other troopers. He kept the booze flowing and spun hair-raising yarns of Indian atrocities. These soldiers were young, had not seen a great deal of action, and did not know just what the savages were capable of. But Drake filled their ears with his blood-drenched tales of rape and murder, and it was not long before they were ready to go out and look for an Indian to kill.

The sergeant bided his time and waited until it was early morning. When he was good and ready, he drained the last of the whiskey in the bottle in front of him, shoved back his chair, and stood up.

"C'mon, Hewlett," he growled to the trooper who was sitting at the table with him. "Get your buddies. We got places to go and things to do."

"Like what, Sarge?" Private Hewlett asked, looking up at Drake with a bleary stare.

"You'll see," Drake replied cryptically. He did not want to tell the others what he had planned, just in case any of them decided to back out. They would be less likely to balk if they thought they were acting on the spur of the moment.

Hewlett put his hands on the table and pushed himself to his feet. He staggered over to the other soldiers and told them, "Sarge says we're leavin'."

One of the men was leaning on the bar, drinking from a bottle. He put it down with a thump and shook his head. "Not ready t'go back t'camp," he slurred.

The other two troopers were busy running their hands over the bar-girls, and they showed even less inclination to leave. Hewlett had no luck getting any of them to come with him. Waiting impatiently at the door, Drake turned and saw the privates ignoring Hewlett.

"Get over here, you bastards!" Drake roared. At his bellow the reluctant troopers leaped to their feet and rushed over. The barman was the only other man in the room, and he watched the show with a bored look on his face.

Drake glowered at the troopers and then said, "Don't you men know that it's after midnight? We're supposed to be back in camp by now."

One of the soldiers muttered an obscenity. The others did not seem to comprehend what Drake was saying.

The sergeant grinned broadly. "I don't reckon ol' Cap'n Hogan is goin' to be waitin' up for us, and I know the fella on guard duty tonight. He ain't goin' to be spreadin' no stories about when we came in. So I guess we can go have us a little more fun."

A ragged cheer went up from the men, and Drake knew that even in their drunken state they would do whatever he wanted. Even if it meant laying waste to that whorehouse where White Elk Duquesne was staying while Drake dealt with the scout himself.

The Gem was on Spruce Street, near the corner of Railroad Avenue. A sidewalk ran along the street, although it was not as elaborate as the boardwalks of Texas Street. With the troopers following behind him, Drake walked onto the planks. The sergeant paused, taking a deep breath and listening to the silence of the sleeping town.

In the stillness he heard the distant clattering of horse's hooves.

It was a lone rider, he judged, moving along one of the streets a couple of blocks north, on the other side of the Kansas Pacific tracks. Some instinct told Drake to wave a hand and hiss a warning at the men with him. Staying in the shadows, he moved toward the sound, squinting through the darkness.

The rider moved across the intersection of Spruce and Third. Drake's breath caught in his throat. Even at this distance, in the gloom, he recognized the tall, lean figure wearing a distinctive broad-brimmed hat.

Duquesne . . .

An expression that was part smile and part grimace tugged at Drake's wide mouth. He would not have to look for Duquesne now. His chance for revenge had just ridden past him, unsuspecting. Although he regretted he no longer had an excuse to start another ruckus at Grace Pinkston's, Drake realized it would be safer to jump Duquesne while the half-breed was alone.

Drake's hands balled into fists, and his heart was pounding. He was going to enjoy teaching Duquesne a lesson.

And if in the process he cheated the renegade called Buffalo Knife of his chance to kill Duquesne . . . Well, he was not going to worry about disappointing some murdering redskin, he thought.

"Keep your goddamn mouths shut and come on," he hissed sharply at his companions. "Any man who makes too much noise will answer to me."

With Drake leading the way, the soldiers scurried down the boardwalk. When they reached Third Street, they turned west and spotted Duquesne walking his horse only a little more than a block ahead of them. Drake motioned them forward and broke into a run. The dust of the street muffled his footsteps.

Exhaustion and his own muddled thoughts prevented White Elk from being as aware of his surroundings as he normally was. At last some instinct warned him that danger threatened, and he straightened abruptly in the saddle and twisted around just as a shadowy form hurtled at him.

Before he could react, the attacker slammed into him, and powerful arms encircled his waist. As his horse shied away, the scout felt himself sliding out of the saddle. One of his feet caught in a stirrup, and he had a frightening vision of being dragged to his death as the animal bolted. But then someone else grabbed him, and his foot wrenched painfully out of the stirrup.

White Elk heard several sets of footsteps as more men surrounded him. The first man still held him in a bear hug. The scout tried to drive an elbow into his opponent's midsection, but it glanced off the man's ribs. White Elk's own ribs, still sore from his tumble down the stairs at Grace's, ached agonizingly as the man increased the pressure on them.

A familiar voice grunted in White Elk's ear, "Help me get the redskinned bastard into that alley over there!"

Drake!

Knowing who his opponent was made White Elk struggle that much harder. There were three or four troopers with the sergeant, and they were able to pull and shove him into the deep shadows of an alley while Drake maintained his painful grip on him.

Once they were in the alley between a store and a warehouse, Drake suddenly ran toward the wall of the warehouse. He planted a hand in the middle of White Elk's back and shoved hard, propelling the scout into the wall with brutal force. White Elk managed to lift his hands to take some of the impact, but he was unable to keep his head from slamming against the bricks. He staggered back as pain exploded behind his eyes.

Struggling to stay upright, White Elk felt a foot thrust between his legs. He fell, landing heavily on a shoulder. Drake loomed over him, growling, "Get him on his feet!"

Two troopers leaned down and grabbed White Elk's arms, jerking him up so abruptly that it felt as if his arms were being torn from their shoulder sockets. He gasped and sagged in the grip of the men, telling himself that he had to fight back but unable to find the strength to do so. The long night had simply drained him of all energy.

"Hang on to him," Drake said. As the sergeant moved in, the scout could see his bunched and ready fists, and he knew what was coming. He tried to tighten his stomach muscles to withstand the blow.

Drake's fist smashed into him like the kick of a mule. White Elk felt the air driven out of his lungs, felt his stomach spasm. There was nothing there, however, since Lora had gone into labor before they had a chance to eat supper, so dry heaves racked White Elk's body. He was not sick for very long. Another punch followed the first one a moment later.

As in the fight at Grace's, the troopers held White Elk while Drake pounded him unmercifully. The scout was in agony from his waist to his shoulders as Drake's big fists slammed into him again and again. Finally, the pain began to ease, only to be replaced by a frightening numbness. White Elk's mind floated up and out of his body so that he could look down on the horrifying scene in the alley.

He was going to die. He knew that. But at least he had gotten to see little Josette before his time was up, and he knew that Lora had come through the birth all right. That was something to hang on to as his grip on his own life slipped away.

From somewhere far away, he heard Drake say, "All right, let the bastard go."

After the troopers released him, he fell for what seemed like an eternity into a long dark chasm. At long last, his face hit the dirt of the alley, and dust was driven into his mouth and nose. He gasped, trying to clear away the dust and drag air into his lungs. He was not dead yet; that fact surprised him.

"I've had my fun," Drake went on. "Reckon it's

time for you boys to have yours. Let's stomp the redskinned heathen good and proper." His laugh was harsh. "You won't be able to do a damn thing for that whore of yours after we get through with you, Duquesne."

He heard Drake laugh again as a booted foot slammed into his body. White Elk was aware of being lifted up slightly by the kick. Then another one hit him, and another. . . .

A vagrant wind spun down the alley, kicking up little dust devils and causing the trash littered there to blow this way and that. A piece of paper skittered along the ground and suddenly stopped against White Elk's face.

Slowly, the scout raised his hand. By the time his fingers reached his cheek, the blood seeping from the cuts had stained the scrap of paper crimson. He fumbled at the paper, pulled it away from his battered features, and then released it to let it blow away on the breeze.

He was alive. God knew how it had happened, but Drake and the others had not killed him.

He moaned. Death might be better than this pain. He felt as if he had been beaten from head to toe.

White Elk lifted his hand a little higher and let his fingers gingerly explore his head. Although the slightest touch set off blasts inside his skull, he decided after a minute that he had no serious injuries there. His face was a mass of cuts and scrapes, and one sore lump had risen on the side of his head, but that was the extent of the damage.

His torso was another story. As he tried to roll over and sit up, he could tell that his taped midsection had been battered and bruised. The muscles refused to work for long minutes, and when he was finally able to pull himself to a sitting position, he almost shrieked at the pain.

But he had made it this far, he thought as he gritted his teeth to hold in the scream. He would make it the rest of the way. Once he was on his feet, he could find help.

The thought of yelling for assistance occurred to him, but he doubted that anyone would hear him at this hour and in this place. His vision was a little blurred, but it was clear enough for him to tell that it was a long while before dawn. The night was as dark as it had been when Drake and his men had jumped him.

To keep his mind off the pain, White Elk wondered what the devil Drake had been doing in town. The cavalry troop had been split in half, and Captain Hogan had been left with barely enough soldiers to man the patrols.

White Elk realized that that detail would not prevent Drake from manipulating Hogan. He had known the sergeant for a long time and had seen Drake maneuver expertly to get his own way. Hogan was still a little unsure of himself, too. The non-com would have been able to talk him into almost anything.

Drake must have come into Abilene looking for him, White Elk saw only too clearly. He had gotten the other troopers liquored up so that they would gladly help him in his quest for vengeance. White

Elk did not understand why they had jumped him in the street. The scout would have expected Drake to come looking for him at Grace's house. . . .

Suddenly, he remembered Rita. Drake had already tried once to assault her. Would he go looking for her now that he was finished with White Elk?

That question galvanized White Elk into action. He lurched to his feet with a grunt, staggered a couple of steps, then righted himself by placing a hand firmly against the warehouse wall. In the faint starlight he saw a dark smear on the wall, and he somehow knew that it was his own blood, which had splattered from his nose when Drake shoved him against the bricks.

He had to warn Rita. That thought echoed through his pain-filled brain. He did not want Rita and Grace and Malachi to suffer because some insane sergeant had a grudge against him.

White Elk forced his legs to work, and he began to stumble out of the alley.

Along Third Street there were only a few hitch-racks, but he staggered between those few for support as he lurched along. No one was on the street, and the houses and businesses he passed were dark. He moved very slowly, but finally he reached Walnut Street and turned toward Grace's, now only a block away.

Lift a leg, wince at the pain, place it in front of the other one, lift again, more pain . . . It was a brutal routine, but White Elk stuck to it. He could see a light burning in the window at Grace's, and he kept his eyes fixed on that warm glow as he stumbled along. He wondered where his horse had gone after Drake and the others had pulled him from the saddle. If it had come back here alone, Rita and Grace would probably be worrying about him.

Well, Grace would be, anyway. Considering how angry Rita had been with him when he left, she might not care what happened to him.

But that did not matter. He would warn her about Drake—

Somehow he made it up the walk to the front door. When he reached it, he leaned against it for a long moment, enjoying the smooth feel of cool wood on his bloody, throbbing face. He fumbled for the knob, found it, turned it, felt the door moving away from him.

He saw the carpeted floor of the foyer rise toward him as he thudded into it. A croak escaped from his throat, a cry of warning and a plea for help combined. He lifted his head, blinked the sweat and blood from his eyes, and saw Grace Pinkston emerge from her office at the end of the hall. She stopped abruptly and lifted her hands to her horrified face.

Grace's scream echoed in the dark chasm that engulfed him.

Chapter Twelve

---◆◇◆---

WHEN MALACHI HEARD GRACE'S SCREAMS, HE CAME running from his room next to the kitchen. Dawn was less than an hour away, and the black man would have been climbing into bed had it not been for the interruption. But Grace's urgent cry had banished any thought of sleep.

Upstairs, only three of the prostitutes still had customers. They clutched at the nervous men and urged them to stay where they were. Malachi would take care of any trouble, the women assured their bed partners. It was better not to get involved. The girls who were not working followed Grace's rule and cowered in their rooms.

All except Rita Nevins. After White Elk had left her room, Rita had seethed angrily throughout the day—even though she knew it was unreasonable to expect anything permanent from him. She was a whore—that was all she ever would be—and he was nothing but a free-drifting scout.

For the first time since White Elk had arrived in Abilene, Rita had considered taking other customers. Some impersonal dallying might take her mind off him, she had thought. But when it was time to join the girls in the parlor, she had stayed in her room and turned in early. Grace had not said anything and left her alone.

However, Rita had not been able to sleep; the fact that White Elk had not returned obsessed her. Where could he be? Surely he had not been at his father's house all this time.

She had tossed and turned, trying futilely to doze off, until Grace's screams tore through the house. Hesitating for only a moment, Rita flung the covers back and leaped to her feet. She raced toward the door, snatching a flimsy robe and tugging it around her nude body as she went, and hurried into the hall.

She heard Grace wail, "Help him, Malachi! Oh my God, help him!"

Rita broke into a run. When she reached the top of the stairs and looked down into the foyer, she saw what she had feared most—the battered, bloody form of White Elk Duquesne sprawled on the carpeted floor, his head cradled in Malachi's lap. Rita flew down the stairs.

Grace had stopped screaming. The madam was standing next to Malachi, her hands still covering part of her face, as she stared down at White Elk. Rita grabbed her arm. "What happened?" she demanded.

"I . . . I heard someone come in the door. . . . When I came out of the office, he was there. . . ."

"Looks like somebody hurt him real bad, Miss Rita," Malachi said.

Grace took a deep breath, visibly regaining control of her emotions. "All right, we'll do what we can for him. Malachi, the sofa in the parlor is the closest place. Can you put him there?"

"Yes, ma'am." Malachi nodded. Gently, he slipped an arm around White Elk's shoulders and another under his legs. The black man straightened and, grunting at the effort, came to his feet. He carried White Elk into the parlor and laid him on the sofa.

Grace turned to Rita. "Get some water and cloths," she ordered. "We'll have to wash away the blood before we can tell how badly he's hurt."

"Shouldn't someone go get Dr. Bloom?"

Grace hesitated. "Not yet," she said. "Pierre doesn't want to draw any more attention to this place than he has to. He's afraid Marshal Travis will try to close us down, especially after all the trouble we've had."

Rita stared in disbelief. "But White Elk is his son. He's hurt! Surely Pierre would want us to help him."

"That's what we are doing," Grace declared, her voice sharper now. "Are you going to get that water?"

"I'll get it," Rita snapped, and struggled to control her anger.

She went to the kitchen and found a basin, then went outside to fill it at the pump. As she pumped the water, Rita glanced at the sky. The first pale streaks of dawn were starting to brighten the eastern horizon. A cool pre-dawn breeze made Rita shiver in her flimsy wrap.

By the time she returned to the parlor, Malachi had removed White Elk's buckskin shirt and pants. Rita gasped and almost dropped the pan of water when she saw the ugly bruises that covered his body. There was hardly an inch of flesh that was not swollen and discolored.

Grace took the water and the cloths and knelt next to the scout. As she began to wipe away the dried blood on White Elk's face, he moaned softly but did not open his eyes.

"Looks like someone beat him within an inch of his life," Malachi said, and shook his head. "Several men must've jumped him without any warning. They couldn't have done this to Mr. Duquesne any other way."

Rita stood watching, hugging herself and remembering the brutal touch of the sergeant called Drake. "I'll bet it was Drake," she said with a shudder. "He'd do this kind of thing."

Without looking up from her task, Grace said, "I think you're right, Rita, but now it doesn't matter who did it. From what I can see, he's in very bad shape." She turned and met Rita's worried gaze. "You'd better go tell Pierre."

"What?" Rita asked in surprise.

"I think you were right. White Elk needs a doctor, but that's Pierre's decision. Like you said, White Elk *is* his son."

Rita nodded slowly. "All right, if you think that's

best." She hurried out of the parlor and started up the stairs. She hated to leave White Elk, but the only way she could help was to do as Grace said. That would be the fastest way to get the medical help he desparately needed.

Unless she went against Grace's wishes and went for Aileen Bloom herself.

As the thought crossed her mind, she knew she could not do it. She had followed Grace's orders for years, and it was too late to start defying her. Besides, Pierre Duquesne had a right to know about his son's injuries.

Hurriedly, Rita began to dress in a simple outfit she seldom wore. Usually she preferred the gaudy garments most girls in her profession favored. While she dressed, she realized that the anger she had felt toward White Elk the day before had vanished.

All she wanted was for him to be all right.

Once clothed, she went quickly down the stairs and paused at the entrance to the parlor. "How is he?" she asked.

Grace and Malachi were still hovering over White Elk. Grace had cleaned most of the blood off his face. Rita could see that the scout's nose was swollen and might well be broken. His breathing was rasping and labored.

"I don't know," Grace said honestly. "I've never seen a man beaten this badly."

"I have," Malachi added. "It's not good, Miss Rita. But they don't seem to have beaten him about the head very much. If he makes it, his brain should be all right."

If he makes it . . . The ominous words made Rita shudder. "I'll be back as soon as I can," she said. She threw a shawl around her shoulders as she hurried to the front door.

She strode quickly, almost ran, down Walnut Street and turned east onto Third. She could have hitched up Grace's buggy, but because she was inexperienced, that would have taken longer than walking to Pierre's house. As she dashed along the street, she watched the eastern sky grow brighter.

In some of the houses she passed, she noticed lanterns burning. Some of Abilene's folk were early risers. There were no horses or wagons moving on Third Street as yet, and Rita was glad. Anyone who saw her would wonder why a prostitute was walking in this neighborhood.

She had never been to Pierre Duquesne's house, but she knew where it was. Even in the pre-dawn shadows, it looked somehow wholesome, not at all like the home of a bordello owner. That had to be the influence of that mousy wife of his. A whoremonger—that was what some people would call Pierre if they knew the truth about him. Rita opened the gate and went up the walk to the porch. Pierre would certainly be surprised to see her, she thought. Hoping not to wake Lora Duquesne if she could avoid it, Rita knocked softly on the front door. When no one answered, she rapped harder. White Elk's life might be at stake, she thought. She decided not to worry too much about being polite at a time like this. As she pounded more loudly on the door, Rita felt her pulse hammering harder as well.

Suddenly the door swung open, startling Rita. A bulky woman with her hair pulled back in a bun glared at her. "Land sakes!" the woman exclaimed. "What's all that noise? Don't you know we've got a new mother and baby here?"

Rita's eyes widened. She knew that Pierre's wife had been pregnant, but she had heard nothing about the baby being born. She gathered her shaken wits and said, "I . . . I need to see Mr. Duquesne."

"He's sleeping," the woman replied curtly. "I'm Mrs. Dawson. I'm here to look after the missus and the baby." She sniffed disapprovingly as she took in Rita's appearance. "Is there anything I can do for you?"

"It's very important that I speak to Mr. Duquesne," Rita insisted, trying to restrain her anger. This woman certainly had no right to judge her under these circumstances. "It could be a matter of life or death."

Mrs. Dawson started to shake her head, but she stopped when heavy footsteps clomped in the hallway behind her. Pierre Duquesne appeared in the doorway and shouldered Mrs. Dawson aside. His head was cocked to one side, and he held a hand pressed against his temple. As he peered at the strawberry blonde standing on his porch, he winced.

"Rita?" he said in disbelief. "Is that you, gal?"

"You know this . . . this woman, Mr. Duquesne?" Mrs. Dawson asked, her voice dripping with contempt.

"Of course I know her," Pierre snarled. He glanced at Mrs. Dawson, then cast a longer, startled look at her. "Who the hell are you, and what are you doing in my house?"

"Why, I'm Alice Dawson. Marshal Travis and Dr. Bloom asked me to come over and help you look after Mrs. Duquesne and the baby."

Pierre's mouth opened and closed, but he did not speak. Finally, he managed to croak, "The baby?"

"That's right. Don't you know you have a beautiful daughter?"

Pierre shook his head and started to turn from the doorway.

Rita moved forward quickly, reached out, and grasped his sleeve. "Mr. Duquesne, I have to talk to you!" she said urgently. "It's about your son White Elk."

Pierre paused, then sneered disgustedly. "I don't have a son," he declared. "Didn't you hear this woman? I've got a child who's all white, instead of some damned trouble-making half-breed whelp."

Rita, stunned by his callous attitude, gaped at him.

"What's the matter with the boy?" he asked harshly. "He come in too drunk to do you any good in bed? Those redskins never could handle whiskey."

"He's hurt," Rita said in a low voice that quivered with rage. "Someone beat him very badly."

For an instant, something like concern flickered in Pierre's eyes, visible even in the half-light of dawn. But then his expression hardened. "It's none of my business anymore," he snapped. "You go back and tend to him, whore. He's your lover, ain't he?"

Speechless, Rita felt the blood draining from her cheeks. It was all she could do not to hurl herself at the arrogant old man and claw his eyes out.

Pierre turned away. "I've got to go see my baby," he said softly as he staggered down the hall. Mrs. Dawson glared at Rita, then slammed the door firmly in her face.

Rita stared at the closed door for a long moment. A shudder went through her, and she convulsively turned away.

Despite what Grace had said, Rita knew that only one course was open to her. She had to find Dr. Bloom and bring her to the house herself. Grace and Malachi would do everything possible for White Elk, but he needed medical attention. If Pierre would not provide it, Rita knew she had to.

She rushed down the walk and hurried toward the heart of town. Surely someone would be out and about, despite the early hour, who could tell her where to find Aileen Bloom.

On the outskirts of Abilene, shadowy silent figures rode ever closer to town. As the riders reached the Smoky Hill River and forded it, the man in the lead headed the band toward a grove of trees and raised his hand to bring them to a halt. To maintain the silence, the renegade called Buffalo Knife motioned to the two dozen men to dismount and gestured to one to stay and watch the horses. The brave nodded grimly.

On foot, Buffalo Knife and his men slipped quickly into town, taking advantage of every bit of cover they could find. His scouts had told him that the yellowleg soldiers were camped on the eastern edge of town, so sentries might well be on duty in Abilene itself. Avoiding the patrols to the south had been fairly easy. All that remained was to find White Elk Duquesne.

Buffalo Knife would kill the hated half-breed himself. Once that was done, he and his men would kill as many of the whites as they could before they themselves were cut down.

It would be a good way to die, Buffalo Knife thought, to be awash in the blood of his enemies.

Sergeant Virgil Drake's head was pounding. He roused from the half-sleep that gripped him and felt around for the bottle he had been drinking from earlier. The sergeant's fingers touched the cool, smooth glass, and he lifted the bottle with a sigh. Whiskey sloshed quietly inside it. Drake raised the neck of the bottle to his mouth and tipped it, swallowing the fiery liquid with relish and then wiping his mouth with the back of his hand.

He was sitting in the recessed doorway of a shop on Buckeye Street. The store was not open yet, and as Drake blinked his eyes and peered around him, he realized that the sun had not yet risen. Gray shadows still cloaked the street.

He knew he was in trouble, but he did not care. The other troopers, as drunk as they had been, had finally realized that they had better return to camp. They had started back an hour or so after having their fun with Duquesne. Private Hewlett had tried to convince Drake to join them, but the sergeant had refused.

Once his score had been settled with that half-breed, Drake had given in to the thirst that had gripped him. He had poured whiskey down his throat until he was drunk. Going back to camp to be chewed out by Captain Hogan was the last thing he wanted to do. Given the mood he was in, he thought he might never go back.

The others had slunk back to Hogan with their tails between their legs. Drake had wandered the streets of Abilene, drinking until he had found this quiet little doorway. It had seemed like a good place to sit down and doze for a while, so that was what Drake had done.

Now it was nearly morning, and within an hour or so, Hogan would have him down as a deserter. Somewhere in the fuzzy reaches of Drake's brain, he realized that he could still make it to camp in time to avoid that. He would certainly get in trouble, might even get busted and draw some time in the stockade, but that was better than being shot. He started to get to his feet.

The sound of footsteps hurrying, almost running, along the boardwalk made him look up suddenly. It would be just his lousy luck to run into that marshal or his hotshot deputy. Drake forced himself to his feet and shook his head to clear some of the cobwebs. He had a headache, and his stomach was a little queasy. Other than that he did not feel too badly, considering how much liquor he had put away.

He huddled against the door of the shop, out of sight of whoever was coming along the boardwalk.

A young woman strode past, her face set in worried lines, her long strawberry-blond hair in attractive disarray, like she had just gotten out of bed.

It was her, Drake realized, the whore from Grace Pinkston's.

Duquesne's whore.

Drake reflexively shot out his arm, and his big hand clamped on Rita Nevins's shoulder. He jerked her around and pulled her closer to him. Leering at her, he clapped his other hand over her mouth to cut off the scream that she was starting to utter.

"Howdy, gal," Drake hissed. "Good to see you again. Sure didn't expect to run into you."

She flinched, her eyes wide with terror and revulsion. Her reaction only added fuel to the fire blazing inside him. Drake tightened his arm around her and ground his groin against her belly.

"Been lookin' forward to meetin' you again," he went on. "I figure it's time you learned what it's like with a real man, 'stead of Injuns and fellas who have to pay for it."

Rita sank her teeth into the palm of his hand. As pain shot up his arm, Drake yelped. Instinctively, he jerked his hand away from her mouth, the flesh tearing as he did so. Drops of red spattered the boardwalk as he shook his wounded hand.

"Goddamn bitch!" he growled. He saw her open her mouth to scream, and his bloody hand flashed up. It cracked across her face and knocked her head to the side.

Drake balled his fist and hit her in the stomach. Rita gasped for air, then retched. Drake whirled her around and slammed her against the side of the doorway. With his injured hand, he grabbed her neck, smearing the soft white skin with crimson. Then he tightened his grip, choking her, while his other hand roamed over her body. His fingers dug cruelly into her breasts.

"I'll show you," Drake panted, swept up in a frenzy of lust and hate. "Show you and that goddamn half-breed both——"

It had to be quick, he thought; people would be moving on the street soon. But he still had time to have his way with her, then slit her throat with his clasp knife. What sweet revenge that would be! When it was done, he would hurry back to camp and trust to luck that he would not be connected with the killing. His luck had to turn.

Rita's knee slammed into his groin. As pain shot through him, Drake uttered a high-pitched, keening wail. When he started to double over, Rita twisted frantically in his grasp and almost slipped away.

Still bent in agony, Drake caught the collar of her dress and flung her back again, smashing her against the wall once more. In a red haze of pain and fury, he fumbled in his pocket and found the knife. Jerking it out, he flicked it open with one hand.

Muttering incoherent curses, Rita swatted at him with both hands. Drake straightened from his crouch and swept her futile blows aside. Then he thrust the hand that held the knife at her.

The blade ripped into her stomach.

Rita sagged back against the wall, her mouth gaping in a soundless scream as Drake tore the knife from her body. Her hands clutched at the wound as blood oozed between her fingers. Her eyes were glazed; her skin ashen.

Seeing the blood on her dress, Drake suddenly was aware of the weight of the knife. He stood numbly staring at her, stunned by what he had done. He had intended to kill her, but not until he had used her for his pleasure. He had cheated himself of that.

Rita began to fall, caught herself as her knees hit the boardwalk, and knelt with her hands pressed to the wound.

Drake's mind began to reel. He had to make sure she was dead before he left, or she might tell someone who had done this to her. He stepped closer, his grip tightening on the handle of the knife. One quick slash across the throat would do it. He would just reach out, grab that thick mane of hair, and yank her head back, exposing her throat—

From the expression on her face Drake could tell that Rita knew what he was going to do. He would have to move fast to prevent her from screaming.

She did not try to scream. Instead she lunged forward, finding the strength somewhere to scoop up the whiskey bottle he had dropped earlier. She stood up and slashed furiously at him with the bottle.

Drake was taken by surprise. He flung up an arm to ward off the blows, and it happened to be the hand which held the knife. The bottle cracked painfully against his wrist. The blade slipped from his fingers and skittered away on the boardwalk.

Rita kept striking at him with the bottle, driving him out of the alcove. The thick glass clunked against Drake's skull, staggering him. His vision blurred, and he almost fell. As he caught himself against the wall of the store, he saw Rita drop the bottle and turn to run.

He wondered how she could move so quickly, as badly wounded as she was. But he had seen men shot to pieces in battle who were still standing long after they should have been dead. A few of them had even miraculously survived.

Drake could not let that happen—the whore had to die. He ran after her.

He paid no attention to where he was; all he could think about was murder and vengeance. He saw Rita duck into an alley and pounded after her.

Drake never reached the alley. Suddenly a figure loomed in front of him in the early morning shadows. The maddened sergeant had only a split second to see the stranger, the bright slashes of paint across his swarthy face, the buckskins the man wore. . . .

For an instant, Drake thought that White Elk Duquesne had come back to haunt him. But this was no half-breed. This apparition in the dawn haze was a full-blooded Kiowa warrior.

Buffalo Knife . . . !

The name flashed through Drake's mind just as something hammered into his back. They were all around him, he realized as he fell to his knees, driven to the dirt of the street by the blow. Somehow, the renegades had slipped through the patrols into Abilene. They had come for their revenge.

Drake broke his fall with his hands before he sprawled onto his face. Trembling, he pushed himself up onto his knees. He glanced around, all thought of the wounded Rita Nevins gone, and saw two dozen warriors surrounding him. To his terror-stricken mind, it looked like a hundred.

But there was only one Buffalo Knife. The Kiowa

leader stared haughtily at Drake. In guttural English he said, "Dog of a yellowlegs soldier! Fate has put you in my hands. Now you will tell me what I want to know."

His heart pounding so hard it seemed loud enough to rouse the whole town, Drake licked his lips and then nodded. "S-sure, Buffalo Knife," he stammered. "I'll tell you anything you want."

An unpleasant smile tugged at Buffalo Knife's mouth. "So you know who I am," he grunted. "Then you know, too, who I want."

"Duquesne!" Drake spat the name.

"Yes. Where is the half-breed, the traitor to the Kiowa?"

Drake's mind was racing. He was not sure where Duquesne was, but he had a pretty good idea. He and the troopers had left the beaten scout alive. Drake was willing to bet that when Duquesne came to, he would have headed for that whorehouse. Drake grasped that hope. He would trade that information for his life.

He looked around to see where he was. Then he said, "Duquesne's at a house a few blocks away. You go up there and turn west—" He pointed up Buckeye Street toward Fourth and continued to babble the directions to Grace Pinkston's house. Finally Buffalo Knife nodded abruptly, and the terrified Drake stopped rambling.

Drake swallowed and summoned up the nerve to say, "There's soldiers camped on the edge of town. I can show you—"

"We know, dog," Buffalo Knife snapped, and contempt curled his lip. He looked at his men. "This one is not worth dirtying my blade."

Drake thought that meant Buffalo Knife was letting him go. Well, he could stand a little disgrace as long as he was still alive. He started to get to his feet, ready to slip out of Abilene before the massacre started.

One of the braves drove a lance into his back. Drake felt the blow, staggered, and looked down incredulously at the bloody iron point emerging from his chest. He opened his mouth to speak, but a great gush of blood choked off the words. Sergeant Virgil Drake collapsed lifelessly in the street.

With a jerk of his head, Buffalo Knife ordered his warriors to follow him. Then he turned and started toward the house where he would find White Elk Duquesne and take the revenge he had craved for so long.

Chapter Thirteen

———◆———

Rita Nevins slumped in agony against the wall of a building. She had never known pain that was so intense. She clutched at the wound in her belly, trying to stop the flow of blood that welled between her fingers.

She rested her head against the rough wooden wall and closed her eyes as she forced herself to keep drawing air into her lungs. It would be so easy to slide to the ground and let death claim her.

She was sure that Drake had fatally wounded her. She had seen men wounded like this before. But this death would not be easy, as if death ever could be. Rita shuddered as she drew a deep breath and felt the blaze in her middle leap higher and higher.

Gradually, one driving thought began to echo

deep in her mind. It cut through the pain and grew louder and more insistent. *She had to warn White Elk.*

Huddled in the shadows of the alley, she had not seen the confrontation between Drake and Buffalo Knife, but she had heard the Kiowa ask questions and had heard Drake's craven, desperate answers. And she had also heard the sound of something—a lance, perhaps—being driven into flesh. It had been followed by a gasp, and Rita knew without looking that the renegades had killed Drake. It was what he deserved, she thought grimly.

She suspected the Indians had gone; everything had been quiet for a while. She had feared they would come after her once they had finished with Drake, but no one had bothered her. Either they had not noticed where she was hiding, or they did not think she was a threat.

None of that mattered now; she knew what she had to do. She had been given a chance, and she would seize it.

She took one faltering step away from the wall and almost fell. Dizzily, she flung out one arm for balance and touched the wooden planks. After a moment, the world began to slow its insane spinning, and the ground felt more solid under her feet. She forced herself to move them—one step, then another, and another. Every time her foot touched the ground, fresh pain racked her. Slipping from the shadows of the alley, she saw Drake's body sprawled in the street, a huge bloodstain on the back. The sight gave her no satisfaction.

Despite the pain, she began to run. She had no

time to waste if she was going to warn everyone at Grace's. If she did not get there before the Indians, she knew all of them would die. Not just White Elk, but Grace and Malachi and all the women who, if not really her friends, were at least her professional sisters.

The dark red stain on the front of her dress was growing, but Rita kept running.

At Grace Pinkston's, Malachi had followed Grace's orders and found a sheet to cover the unconscious man on the sofa. They had done all they could for White Elk. Grace chewed her lower lip as she looked down at the scout. She wished that Rita would hurry back with Pierre. Pierre would know what to do. He always did.

When Pierre Duquesne had arrived in Abilene several years earlier, the house had been on the verge of going out of business. He had money to spend, and Grace had been glad to take it. She had discovered, though, that Pierre was not content to spend his cash in the usual way. He wanted to buy into the business. Grace had allowed herself to be persuaded, and it was not long before Pierre owned the establishment. He had funneled a small fortune into the place; it was only right that he control it as well. Grace had never asked where the money came from; she had not wanted to know.

But ever since that time, she had turned to Pierre for advice, for action when it was needed. It was required now, and she wished he were here.

White Elk let out a groan.

Malachi, who had been sitting in a chair, stood

up quickly and hurried to the sofa. "He's coming to," he said as he watched White Elk's head toss from side to side. The scout shifted and moaned once more.

Grace knelt beside the sofa. "It's all right, White Elk," she said in a gentle voice. "You're safe now. You're here at my house."

White Elk's eyes stayed closed, but his mouth opened. "R-Rita . . . ?" he asked in a hoarse voice.

"No, it's me, Grace. Malachi's here, too. Rita has gone for your pa."

White Elk began to blink, and finally he opened his bloodshot eyes. He peered fuzzily at Grace and Malachi and mumbled, "Rita . . . gone for my pa?"

"That's right."

For a long moment, White Elk was silent. Then, to Grace and Malachi's astonishment, he began to laugh. He winced as the laughter shook him, but he could not seem to stop.

At last the spasms subsided, and White Elk said weakly, "You don't really think Pa gives a damn, do you?"

Grace frowned. "He might just surprise you, you know."

White Elk shook his head. "Nothing Pierre Duquesne does surprises me anymore."

He started trying to pull himself into a sitting position. Grace warned him not to exert himself, but he waved away her words of caution. "Give me a hand, Malachi," he said. The black man slipped an arm around his shoulders and supported him as White Elk sat up. The scout clutched the sheet around him and went on, "I could use my clothes."

"What for?" Grace demanded. "You're not going anywhere."

"Yes, I am." White Elk nodded, more to himself than to them. "Got to find another place to stay. Can't live here anymore. . . ."

He was delirious, Grace suddenly realized.

White Elk swung his legs off the sofa and leaned forward, pausing to catch his balance before he tried to stand up. "If you won't get my clothes, I'll get them myself," he declared.

"Help him get his clothes on," Grace told Malachi. When he looked dubiously at her, she snapped, "It's better than having him staggering around, probably falling, and hurting himself even more."

Malachi nodded. He retrieved White Elk's buckskins from the floor where he had dropped them and started gently easing them on the dazed scout.

When White Elk was dressed, Grace brought him a glass of whiskey. She did not know if he should be drinking in his condition, but the alcohol might help dull the pain. White Elk swallowed greedily, shuddered, then winced. When he looked up and met Grace's gaze, his eyes were clearer and more alert.

"Thank you for helping me," he said. "I ran into Sergeant Drake again."

"We figured as much," Malachi grunted. "He had help, too, didn't he?"

"He had . . . a few friends with him," White Elk admitted with a tight grin. He held one hand across his middle, keeping pressure on it so that the pain could not overwhelm him. Having his ribs taped had probably saved him from even worse injury. "I think I'll be all right, though."

"Yes, in a month or so," Grace said dryly.

White Elk held out his empty glass. "Maybe a little sooner if I could have some more of that."

As Malachi grinned and picked up the whiskey bottle, something thumped against the front door.

Grace's head snapped up. If Rita was back with Pierre, she would not have knocked; she would have just come in. But that had not sounded like someone knocking; it had been more like something falling—

"Something's out there," she said tensely. "I'll go see what it is."

"Wait a minute," White Elk said. "Maybe it's Drake coming to cause more trouble."

Malachi stood up. "I'll go check, Miz Grace."

Before either of them could stop him, Malachi strode into the foyer and went to the front door. His fists were bunched and ready, and he looked like he would relish the opportunity to trade punches with Virgil Drake. White Elk forced himself to his feet and went to the parlor doorway. Grace hovered beside him.

As Malachi jerked open the front door, all three of them were surprised once more in this long night of horror.

Rita's huddled body fell heavily onto the carpeted floor and twisted to land on her back. Her hands were laced together over her stomach, and a huge bloodstain was spread around them.

"Rita!" White Elk cried. Grace was too shocked to utter a sound.

Malachi dropped to his knees beside Rita as White Elk shakily rushed forward. The black man carefully lifted Rita's hands from her belly. He grimaced as he looked at the wound.

"Somebody tore her open with a knife," he said, and glanced up at White Elk.

"Well, do something for her!" White Elk exclaimed.

Slowly, Malachi shook his head. "There's nothing I can do, nothing anybody can do," he said solemnly. "She's lost too much blood, Mr. Duqucsne."

White Elk knelt beside her, his own pain forgotten. Grace moved behind him and peered over his shoulder at Rita's ashen face. With Malachi's help, the scout slipped an arm around Rita's shoulders and lifted her so that her head was pillowed on his lap.

Her eyes flickered open, and she looked up at White Elk. In a voice that was little more than a whisper, she said, "You . . . you're all right. . . ."

"I'm fine," White Elk told her. He had forgotten about the pounding in his head, the bands of pain around his torso. All of his attention was focused on Rita. "Who did this to you?"

Rita licked her lips. "D-Drake . . ."

Fury surged through White Elk. "Drake! I'll kill him!"

Rita's fingers plucked weakly at his sleeve. "I . . . I've got to tell you—"

"Just rest right now," White Elk broke in. "We'll get help for you."

Rita shook her head and drew on all her reserves. "Listen . . . to me . . . dammit!" she gasped. "There's an Indian . . . coming here. . . . Drake

told him where to find you.... He killed
Drake—"

"Drake's dead? Who did it?"

"B-Buffalo ... Knife ... I think that's what
Drake called him. . . ."

A shudder went through her body, and blood
trickled from the corner of her mouth. Her green
eyes stared at White Elk, and he saw death in them.
He wanted to lift her to his chest, crush her against
him.

"I . . . love . . ." Her final words were a soft
breath. Then she was silent, and her eyes stared
sightlessly at the foyer ceiling.

A heart-wrenching spasm tore through White
Elk. He closed his eyes and dropped his head. He
had thought there was no real love between him
and this soiled dove called Rita. He had been
wrong.

But Buffalo Knife was on his way, and he had no
time to dwell on regrets. He opened his eyes and
looked up to meet Malachi's grim gaze. "You and
the others have to get out of here, fast," White Elk
said. "Buffalo Knife and his renegades will be here
any minute."

Malachi shook his head, and Grace put a hand
on White Elk's shoulder. "What about you?" she
asked.

"I'll stay here," White Elk said bleakly, all emo-
tion gone from his voice. "I can hold them off for a
few minutes, give you a chance to get away and
warn the town."

"Not by yourself," Malachi declared. He stood
up. "Come on, Miz Grace. You go rouse the girls
and get them out of here."

"We . . . we can't just leave you two here—" Grace began.

"That's all you can do," White Elk said. He eased Rita's head onto the carpet and stood up. He turned to Malachi. "Have you got some rifles here?"

The black man nodded. "I'll fetch them."

Grace started to protest, but White Elk stopped her with a shake of his head. "Buffalo Knife will kill all of you if you don't get out of here," he said grimly. "You don't want that happening to your girls, do you?"

Grace shook her head. Her eyes glistened with tears. "I'll go get them," she said.

She hurried up the stairs while Malachi came back to the foyer. He was carrying several rifles and a couple of boxes of ammunition. "It looks like you were expecting trouble," White Elk commented.

"Nope," Malachi said with a shake of his head. "I don't believe in being caught by surprise."

White Elk's mouth stretched in a humorless grin as he took one of the Winchesters from Malachi and began to load it. When they had filled all the magazines, White Elk leaned the last of the rifles against the wall and bent to pick up Rita. Cradling her body in his arms, he carried her into the parlor and lay her on the sofa where he had rested earlier. He knew he was operating on sheer willpower, refusing to acknowledge the pain that racked his body.

He pulled the sheet over Rita and lingered long enough to gently stroke her cheek. Then he returned to the foyer, picked up two rifles, and moved to the windows in the parlor. Flicking the heavy curtain aside, he peered outside. In the early morning light, he could see no one moving on the street.

Grace stepped into the parlor and said, "The girls and the few customers who were here are leaving through the back door right now, White Elk. Malachi looked around first and didn't see anyone, so maybe we'll make it."

White Elk turned from the window. He reached out and took Grace's hand. "Good luck," he said fervently. "I'm sorry I brought you this trouble. I never should have come to Abilene."

Grace smiled. "Hell. You've made things interesting." She squeezed his hand and then hurried down the hall toward the kitchen and the back door.

Looking out the window, White Elk scanned the early morning shadows on the street. A few minutes later, Malachi joined him and said, "I think Grace and the others got away all right. I kept an eye on them until they slipped over to Elm Street. Grace said she'd tell Marshal Travis what's happening."

"Once Buffalo Knife gets here, I've got a feeling Travis will know what's going on," White Elk said grimly.

He had barely spoken the words when a bullet punched through the window, shattering it and spraying glass across the room. White Elk ducked instinctively, then crouched below the sill. He edged his head up as a rifle cracked in the street. Another slug thudded into the outside wall of the house.

White Elk saw the warriors advancing toward the house, scurrying from tree to tree. He stood up, flung the Winchester to his shoulder, and squeezed off a shot. The bullet whined beside one of the running shadows, close enough to make the brave throw himself to the ground and hunt for cover. White Elk searched for Buffalo Knife but did not see the Kiowa leader. But he knew he was out there.

Malachi crouched at another window. Taking deliberate aim, he fired twice, then said, "We'd better make our shots count. Looks like there are quite a few of them."

As he watched for another target, White Elk nodded. He had seen eight or nine warriors, which meant there were at least twice that many. He and Malachi could not hold out for long. They would be killed—but he would make Buffalo Knife pay a high price first.

Cody Fisher was in the marshal's office when the shooting started. He had been on duty since midnight, and he was tired. But the sound of gunfire coming from somewhere north of Texas Street instantly galvanized him. He ran from the office and vaulted onto his pinto, which was tied at the hitchrack.

Spurring the horse to a run, Cody galloped down Texas Street. A few people were on the boardwalk, and they gaped at the deputy as he flashed by. Cody tried to pinpoint the location of the shooting. There was a lot of it now, rifles cracking with ominous regularity.

As Cody reached the intersection of Texas and Walnut, he saw Luke Travis running down the boardwalk, heading in the same direction as his deputy. Travis was hatless. His shirttail flapped outside his pants. But his gun belt was strapped on, and the Colt was in his hand. He lifted his other arm to hail Cody.

Cody reined in next to the boardwalk. Travis rasped, "Where's the shooting coming from?"

Cody started to shake his head, then instead he pointed up Walnut Street. "I'd say it's coming from up there a few blocks."

Travis nodded grimly. "From Grace Pinkston's, maybe. Looks like Buffalo Knife showed up after all."

As soon as he had stopped speaking, Travis heard someone frantically calling his name. He and Cody looked down Texas Street to see Grace Pinkston hurrying toward them, followed by a group of young women in varying stages of undress.

Grace ran up to the two lawmen. She was haggard and breathless, and Travis grabbed her arm to steady her. "What is it?" the marshal asked urgently. "Trouble at your place?"

"Indians!" Grace gasped. "They . . . they've come for White Elk!"

Travis nodded grimly. "That's what I thought." He turned to Cody and ordered, "Head for the cavalry camp. They ought to be awake already, considering all the shooting that's going on. Bring them to Grace's."

"What are you going to do?" Cody asked as he wheeled his horse around.

"I'm going to try to help White Elk," Travis replied flatly.

Cody nodded, knowing that it would do no good to argue with Travis. The best way he could help now was to follow the marshal's orders. He dug his heels into his horse's flanks and shouted as the animal surged forward.

Travis, his keen eyes scanning the yards and houses, ran up Walnut Street. He spotted the shadowy figures advancing on the house while he was still two blocks away. Darting across the street, he cut through an alley to Elm Street and raced along it, paralleling Walnut.

The marshal circled the stable behind Grace's and pounded toward the back door. He saw no sign of Indians here; the renegades were concentrating their attack on the front of the house. Simple and direct, that seemed to be the way Buffalo Knife operated, although the Kiowa was very cunning, Travis thought. He suspected that Buffalo Knife had planned for the majority of the cavalry forces to be decoyed to the western part of the state.

As he reached the house, Travis had no more time to speculate. He slipped into the bordello and catfooted down the hall toward the parlor. He heard rifles firing inside the front room.

As he entered the parlor, Travis glanced through a window and saw one of the warriors running toward the house. The renegade carried a torch, and the lawman realized that he intended to smash the fiery brand through the window. Instinctively, Travis flung his gun up and snapped off a shot.

The bullet shattered the window from the inside and caught the Indian in the chest, knocking him backward. The torch spun out of his hands.

White Elk and Malachi, startled by the shot fired behind them, whirled around. Both men were about to fire when they saw who the newcomer was.

His finger still tight on the trigger, White Elk forced himself to relax slightly. He said, "You ought to be careful about sneaking up on people, Marshal."

"Wasn't time to send you a letter saying I was coming," Travis said dryly as he dropped into a crouch beside the window he had shot out. He squeezed off another round toward the attacking Indians.

White Elk returned his attention to the yard in front of the house and noticed that the fallen torch had started a small grass fire. He saw the sprawled body of the Indian and said, "Thanks, Marshal. That one might have slipped past us."

"He won't be the only one to try to set fire to the house," Travis said. "Here come a couple more!"

A volley of gunfire came from the renegades as two torch-carrying braves ran forward. Travis, White Elk, and Malachi had to duck beneath the windows to keep from being cut to ribbons by the hail of bullets. One of the torches sailed through an already-broken window, setting the curtains afire as it did so. The torch bounced on the carpet, which quickly began to smolder.

"We've got to get out of here!" Malachi exclaimed. "We can't fight the fire and the Indians at the same time!"

Travis knew that was true. He said, "When I came in, there weren't any renegades out back. Let's run for it!"

It was a slim chance, but all three men knew it was the only one they had. They leaped up, fired a last volley through the shattered windows, then raced for the rear of the house.

Travis was the last one to leave the parlor. He

cast a final glance through the smoke and flames toward the window and saw riderless horses, driven by a lone warrior, coming up Walnut Street. Several Indians were already springing onto the horses' backs.

As he raced toward the back door, Travis had to give Buffalo Knife credit for good strategy. He had slipped into town unseen, driven his quarry out of hiding, and now was ready to administer the final blow.

Malachi went through the back door first. He had taken only three steps when a bullet slammed into his thigh. As he cried out in pain, he fell. White Elk was right behind him. He glanced over to see the Indians riding around the corner of the house, their rifles blasting. Travis triggered off a couple of quick shots as he emerged from the house, but he could see that it was too late to flee. In a matter of seconds the renegades would have them trapped against the back of the house.

A Winchester cracked from the stable, shot after shot rolling out as fast as the rifleman could lever shells into the weapon's chamber. The bullets sent two of the Indians flying from their saddles and made the others veer back toward the street.

"Come on!" Pierre Duquesne shouted from the stable door, the Winchester smoking in his hands.

Stunned, White Elk spent a precious second staring at his father, wondering where he had come from. But then he stooped and grabbed Malachi's arm. He hauled the black man to his feet and flung his arm around his waist to support him. Then, taking advantage of Pierre's covering fire, they hurried toward the stable.

Travis fired his Colt at the warriors as he ran after White Elk and Malachi. The three men ducked into the stable while Pierre kept shooting. The marshal opened the cylinder of his gun, dumped out the empty cartridges, and started thumbing fresh ones from his belt into it. "I don't know what you're doing here, Duquesne," he said as he worked, "but I'm mighty glad to see you."

"Grace came and told me my boy was trapped in there, Marshal," Pierre grated. "I got here as soon as I could."

White Elk heard his father's words as he eased Malachi into a sitting position against the stable wall. Glancing at Pierre, he said, "You left Lora and the baby?"

"That Dawson woman's there," Pierre replied. His rifle was empty. He dug in his coat pocket and drew out a handful of shells. As he reloaded, he went on, "Lora and Josette will be all right. That little gal's a real beauty."

White Elk stared, surprised by the unexpected warmth he heard in Pierre's voice. He seemed completely sober.

Travis, his face grimy with gunpowder, grinned broadly. "It sounds like congratulations are in order, Duquesne. Sorry I can't deliver them under better circumstances."

White Elk put a hand on Pierre's arm. "Pa . . . ?"

Pierre pointed his rifle toward the bordello. Flames were now visible through the rear windows as the conflagration began to spread. The Indians had withdrawn for the moment, but everyone in the stable knew that at any moment they would attack again. Without looking at White Elk, Pierre said quietly, "I'm sorry, son . . . sorry about a lot of things. Lora told me how you probably saved her and the baby. Guess they've taught me quite a bit this morning."

White Elk nodded and swallowed the lump that was rising in his throat. "That's good, Pa," he said. "I . . . I just never understood why you always hated me."

Pierre glanced at him. "Hell, boy, I never hated you. I just wanted you to be tough. I knew how the world was going to treat you. You're a half-breed. I figured it was my duty to make you as hard as you could be." Suddenly, he smiled. "Don't know if I succeeded, but you seem like a pretty good man to me."

Blinking back the tears that were welling in his eyes, White Elk looked toward the house. The roof was starting to burn. Rita was in there, in the midst of the inferno. She deserved a spectacular funeral pyre, he thought, and that was what she was getting. His only regret was that Virgil Drake had died at another man's hands.

"Here they come!" Pierre yelled. His Winchester began to explode once more.

Suddenly, he cried out in pain and spun backward; blood blossomed on his shirt. White Elk had time to cast one despairing glance at his father before he began firing at the charging renegades. Then everything was lost in thundering gunfire and a smoking haze.

White Elk stood next to Luke Travis in the stable doorway, both men firing as fast as they could. Malachi had crawled over and joined them. Sprawled on the earth, he had lifted himself on one arm and was firing his rifle with the other hand. Buffalo Knife's men, shooting and whooping wildly, swarmed around both sides of the flaming bordello.

All of a sudden more Indians were flying off their horses than the three men in the stable could account for. The sound of new, approaching hoofbeats slowly reached the battle-weary trio. As a bugle blared, cavalry troopers galloped from behind the stable and met the charging renegades head-on.

Travis, White Elk, and Malachi lowered their guns as the Indians' attack was broken as abruptly as it had begun. Most of the renegades turned and tried to flee, only to be cut down by the fire of Captain Hogan's men.

But one of the warriors did not run. His face twisted with hate and rage, Buffalo Knife plunged his horse toward the stable at a gallop. There was a pistol in his hand, and as he charged he fired it wildly.

White Elk saw him coming. The scout did not know how many shots were left in his rifle, but moving calmly and efficiently, he lifted it to his shoulder. Buffalo Knife's hatred of him had caused untold deaths. Now it was time to end it.

Slugs whirled around White Elk's head as Buffalo Knife closed in on him. The scout pressed the trigger of the Winchester and felt the solid kick of the stock against his shoulder as it blasted. He levered, fired again, levered, fired again, until the rifle was empty.

Through the sight of the Winchester, he saw Buffalo Knife's crazed face transform into a crimson mass. The Kiowa was flung off his horse. He landed heavily, rolled over twice, and lay still.

The scout drew a deep breath and slowly lowered the Winchester. It was finally over, he thought. He listened to the fading sound of gunshots. The cavalry and the remaining renegades were fighting a running battle, but the leaderless Indians would be cut down rapidly.

Luke Travis walked out of the stable and prodded Buffalo Knife's corpse with his foot. The Kiowa was dead. The marshal looked up as Cody rode into the yard on his pinto. Travis grinned and said, "You and those soldiers got here just in time. Thanks."

"Not quite in time," Cody said grimly, nodding toward the stable. Travis turned to see White Elk kneeling beside his father's sprawled form.

Pierre looked up at White Elk with pain-filled eyes. The bullet had slammed into his chest. A cough racked him, and blood foamed on his lips. He said in a choked voice, "It . . . it's up to you now, son. You've got to . . . got to take care of Lora and the baby. . . ."

White Elk, blinking back tears, put his hand on Pierre's shoulder and squeezed hard. "No, Pa, that's your job," he said.

"I . . . won't be here . . . to do it," Pierre gasped. "Take . . . take care of yourself . . . too. . . ."

His head sagged to the side.

After a long moment, White Elk slowly released his grip on his father's shoulder. "All right, Pa," he said softly.

Wearily, he stood up and went over to Malachi, who extended a hand to him. White Elk helped the black man to his feet and put an arm around

Malachi's waist to support him. Then they walked out of the stable toward Travis and Cody.

At that moment the roof of the bordello collapsed, sending a huge flurry of sparks into the morning sky. One of them seemed to glow particularly brightly, and White Elk watched it until it was lost in the rays of the rising sun.

Chapter Fourteen

A WEEK LATER, ALMOST ALL TRACES OF THE INDIAN raid had been erased from Abilene. The soldiers had stayed to help clean up, and all that remained of the battle were the smoke-blackened stone walls of Grace Pinkston's gutted house.

The funerals were over, and the dead had been buried. Most of the town had turned out for Pierre Duquesne's service. Sergeant Virgil Drake had been buried with a minimum of ritual. Over the protests of some of the townspeople, Buffalo Knife and his renegades had been buried in Abilene's cemetery. The reservation they had escaped from was too far away for the bodies to be transported back. And White Elk Duquesne was leaving Abilene.

As he waited on the platform of the Kansas

Pacific depot, he chafed at the uncomfortable new suit he was wearing. Next to him stood Lora, holding little Josette in her arms. The baby was wrapped in a blanket, and only her tiny face was visible.

Luke Travis, Cody Fisher, Aileen Bloom, and Orion McCarthy were also standing on the platform. They had come to see White Elk and Lora off. Cody said with a smile, "I don't know how you're going to feel about the East, White Elk. From what I've heard, it's very different from life here on the frontier."

White Elk ran a finger around the collar of his shirt. "I've heard the same thing," he told the deputy. "But I promised my pa I'd take care of Lora and Josette."

"We'll be back," Lora said with a sad smile. "I . . . I couldn't bear to stay in Abilene right now."

"I can understand that," Aileen said. "You've had a hard time, Lora, but I'll bet things will be better in the future."

Lora nodded. "I think you're right." She smiled down at Josette as the baby stirred.

White Elk and Aileen had tried to convince Lora to wait a little longer before traveling, but Lora had been adamant in her desire to leave Abilene. White Elk could not blame her. All he could do was go along and try his best to make sure she was all right.

Someday, though, he had vowed, both Lora and Josette would see the real frontier for themselves. He had a feeling they would find some land out there somewhere, a place where a widow and her child could settle down and make a new start. Maybe an old Army scout could be part of that. . . .

Travis put a hand on White Elk's shoulder and drew him away from the others. Pitching his voice low, Travis asked, "You didn't tell her anything about Grace and your father, did you?"

White Elk shook his head. "No need for her to know," he whispered. "Pierre tried to be a good man, there at the end. She can remember him that way. I know I'm going to try to."

Travis nodded. "Glad to hear it."

"Grace is leaving town, too. She said she and her girls would start over somewhere else. It's going to be hard for them, but she didn't want to stay here either."

"That property where the house was might fetch a pretty good price. Do you want me to look into that for you?"

White Elk grinned. "I'd appreciate that, Marshal. Anything we can get out of it goes to Lora and Josette, of course, but I'd like to handle the matter as quietly as possible."

"Sure." Travis looked down the track to the west and returned White Elk's grin. "Looks like the train's coming."

A moment later, the sound of the whistle reached the platform, bringing with it the promise of a new life.

After the train had pulled out, taking White Elk and Lora and Josette with it, Travis strolled back to the office. The marshal looked up and down the street, noting with satisfaction that the town seemed to be back to normal. Folks were going about their business as usual.

The only thing out of the ordinary were the

soldiers sitting on their mounts in front of the marshal's office.

Captain Hogan nodded to Travis as the lawman walked up. "I just wanted to let you know that we're pulling out now, Marshal," Hogan said. "We'll be heading back to headquarters."

"I hope the next time we see you it won't be during an Indian fight, Captain," Travis said.

Hogan shook his head. "I don't think you'll have any more trouble like that. This business with Buffalo Knife was just an isolated incident. By and large, this part of the country has been pacified."

Travis had to grin wearily at the young officer's smug assertion. "That may be true about the Indians," he acknowledged. "But in Abilene it seems like things are never peaceful for long."